Flight of the Doves

Walter Macken was born in Galway in the West of Ireland in 1915. A hero of Irish literature, he wrote for adults and children, for radio, television and the stage and he also produced plays. He is perhaps best known for his adult novels, which span generations of Irish history from the arrival of Cromwell in Ireland to the Famine.

Island of the Great Yellow Ox, his first children's book, came late in Walter Macken's life and was published in 1964. *Flight of the Doves* followed a couple of years later and was published in 1968, shortly after his death.

Flight of the Doves

Walter Macken

MACMILLAN CHILDREN'S BOOKS

First published 1968 by Macmillan and Company Ltd

This edition published in 2001 by Macmillan Children's Books
a division of Macmillan Publishers Limited
20 New Wharf Road, London N1 9RR
Basingstoke and Oxford
Associate companies throughout the world
www.panmacmillan.com

ISBN 978-0-330-39787-2

13 15 17 19 18 16 14 12

A CIP catalogue record for this book is available from the British Library.

Typeset by Intype Libra Ltd
Printed and bound in the UK by CPI Mackays, Chatham ME5 8TD

Chapter One

Finn made up his mind on an April afternoon. Uncle Toby helped to make it up for him. It was half past six. Uncle Toby came home at about seven o'clock. He would leave the solicitor's office where he worked, go into the Red Dragon, drink some beer and then come home for his high tea, lifting his bowler hat on the way to greet the ladies, exchanging banter with the men. He was tubby, and cheerful looking. He had a broad fat face in which his eyes seemed lost and appeared to twinkle. But they rarely twinkled for Finn or his little sister Derval.

Finn closed his copy book. He had been doing his school lessons. He put them away in his schoolbag. It was a fat bag now because he was twelve and the older you got the more books you had to have. He went to the cupboard and took out the delft and laid the three places at the table. It was an ordinary wooden kitchen table which should have been scrubbed white, but since his mother died two years ago it had never been the same. Finn could never get it as clean as it used to be.

He stirred up the coal fire in the range. The big black kettle was boiling so he put it on one side and put on the pan. On the pan he intended to put rashers and sausages and pudding, because Toby was a lover of fried things, which might be the reason that he was so fat.

1

He put dripping on the pan and was going to get the other things from the cupboard when the door opened and Uncle Toby came in and looked around him. The front door opened straight on to the pavement of the street, and right into the kitchen.

He closed the door.

'Well, young Finn,' he said. 'We are a bit lazy today, boy. The tea is not ready.'

'You don't come home until seven,' said Finn. He knew he shouldn't have said it as soon as it was out of his mouth. He should have said: I am sorry Uncle Toby.

'We are impertinent again,' said Uncle Toby. He hung his bowler hat on the banister knob and came over to Finn. Finn was tensed up, waiting for what was to come.

One of the small fat hands caught hold of his arm, a surprisingly strong grip for such a small hand.

Finn was tall for his age. He could look levelly into the eyes of Uncle Toby. Uncle Toby obviously didn't like what he saw there.

'We must learn not to be impertinent, boy,' he said and slapped him on the face. It was quite a hard slap, but Finn kept looking into his eyes. He didn't show fear. He didn't show pain. He knew this was wrong too, as it only infuriated Uncle Toby.

The slaps on the face came as regularly as the beating of a clock. The repetition of them made his face sore, but he kept looking into Uncle Toby's eyes, seeing how small they were and how mean they were. He didn't like Uncle Toby. He wasn't strong enough to resist so he just stood and took the slaps that were jolting his head.

It was the crying of Derval that stopped it.

She had been playing upstairs. Now she came down and stood there and started to cry and said, 'Stop! Stop! Stop!' Derval was seven. She had long fair hair tied with a ribbon. Finn didn't know why she had fair hair when his own hair was red.

Uncle Toby went over to her.

'We mustn't be a crybabby,' Uncle Toby said, 'or we will be smacked. You hear that.' He caught her by the shoulder. She shrank from him. It was the sight of this that made up Finn's mind for him.

'Don't touch her, Uncle Toby,' he said. He had come forward a few paces. He was holding the heavy iron pan in his hand. Uncle Toby turned to look at him. He looked from his face to the whiteness of his knuckles gripping the pan.

'You have a lot to learn, boy,' he said.

'Just don't touch her,' said Finn. 'Stop crying, Derval.'

She stopped crying.

'You know there are reform schools for boys who attack people with blunt instruments?' Uncle Toby asked.

'Just don't touch her,' said Finn.

Suddenly Uncle Toby became a gentleman again. He relaxed.

'It's come to a pass where a man can't chastise children without threatened assault.' He moved to the basket armchair near the radio set and took the evening paper from his pocket. 'Get on with the cooking,' he said.

Finn put the pan back on the range. He had spilled some of the melted dripping on the floor. He put more on the pan. Derval came from the stairs and got a basin and water from the tap at the

3

sink and went and mopped up the grease with a cloth.

Uncle Toby watched them over the top of the newspaper.

'Why can't you realize how much I have done for you?' he asked. 'When your father died I married your mother. How many men do you think would take on the responsibility of a widow-woman and two small children? Have you thought of that? I gave up a free and easy life to support your mother and you two. I could have had a good time for myself. I didn't have to work and slave to bring up children that were not even related to me. I expect a little gratitude, boy, not impertinence, not insults. Reform yourself, or I will have you reformed if I can't do it myself.'

Feeling that he had re-established himself, he ruffled the paper determinedly and went back to the reading of it. The children were silent.

'I suppose it's the bad Irish blood in you,' he said as an afterthought, and went back to his reading again.

Finn looked at Derval. She was pale. She was making the tea in the brown pot.

Finn remembered his own father only faintly. A cheerful man with red hair, a really cheerful one. He remembered his mother better. She was like Derval, with fair hair. He remembered Uncle Toby too. Uncle Toby had been a lodger with his father and mother, living in the small spare room. It was what he said about Irish blood that determined Finn on the course he would take. He felt impatient now, impatient for the tea to be over, impatient for Uncle Toby to go out again to the pub where he spent his evenings. He

4

forced down this impatience and set himself to the cooking of the tea.

They sat at the table. Uncle Toby invoked the grace of God on their meal. He looked very pious while he did this. They began to eat their meal silently.

Finn looked across at Derval. He felt sorry for her. She was a cheerful little girl. She just wanted people to be nice. He was sorry that their mother was dead on her account. There was very little laughter with Uncle Toby. Before that there used to be lots of laughing. His mother would tell them stories about strange things that had happened to her. All the time her eyes would be laughing. You knew that what she was telling was only a story, but you believed it while she was talking.

Uncle Toby wiped his mouth.

'You will wash up,' he said. 'You will bring in coal. You will break sticks. You will see your sister is in bed and you are not to go out on the streets. You will be in bed before I come back.'

All these things Finn would have done anyhow. He didn't reply.

Uncle Toby rose and put on his bowler hat and walked firmly to the door. He turned there.

'Watch your behaviour, boy,' he said. 'I don't have to hold on to either of you. There are schools and places where you can be put. Don't forget that. And don't think that I wouldn't put you there.'

On this note he departed, and Finn allowed the muscles of his stomach to relax.

Now, he thought, with a bit of luck, it will be a good long time before we see Uncle Toby again.

He looked across at Derval. She was crying silently. He always found it was better to be gruff with her when she was crying.

5

'Derval,' he said, 'please stop crying and dry your eyes. I have something to say to you.'

He watched her. She made a great effort. She raised the hem of her dress and wiped her eyes. Then she looked at him.

'Now, Finn,' she said.

'We are going to run away,' he said.

Her eyes widened.

'Where?' she asked.

'You don't remember the time Mammy and Daddy brought us on a holiday to see our grandmother. You were too young.'

'It was on a boat,' she said.

'You remember that?'

'That's all,' she said.

'It's enough,' he said. 'Now listen. You go upstairs and take all the books out of your schoolbag and put in all your clothes from the drawer into the bag. Can you do that?'

'Oh, yes,' she said. 'This will be an adventure.'

'Yes,' he said. 'We want to be gone by the time Uncle Toby comes home. He won't know until the morning that we are gone.'

'Oh,' she said. 'Will he chase us?'

'I don't know,' said Finn. 'Maybe he will say good riddance to bad rubbish.'

'If he catches us, will he put us into that old school?' she asked.

'No,' said Finn grimly. 'Nobody will separate us. I don't know how, but they won't.'

'Will I go and do it now, so?' she asked, rising from the chair.

'Do,' said Finn. 'Good girl. I'll tidy up down here.'

She ran up the stairs.

He cleared the delft from the table and put them into the sink and ran hot water on them. The details of what he was going to do were clear in his mind, but the actual carrying out of them was a bit hazy. Once they got on the way, it would unfold, he felt sure, like one of his mother's stories that she made up as she went along.

He had the dishes washed and dried when Derval came down the stairs with her schoolbag. She had it stuffed with clothes.

'Is that good?' she asked.

He examined it. 'We can get more into it,' he said. He went up the stairs with her again. There were two bedrooms up there. The big one where Uncle Toby slept and the back one where he and Derval slept in two bunks, one on top of the other. Her clothes were in nursery drawers, painted blue with small coloured teddy-bears painted on them. She had created some confusion pulling things out. He went through them all again. He discarded some things, and packed in other things.

'Can I bring my teddy?' she asked. This tattered teddy was on her pillow. She had had it for many years. It was hardly distinguishable as a teddy now, lacking one eye, and some stuffing in the left leg. He was going to discard it, but he relented at the look in her eyes.

'All right,' he said, 'but just that. You can carry it. Now dress yourself in these slacks, and put on all the jerseys you have, one over another, because it will be cold where we are going. Will you do that?'

'Yes,' she said.

'I'll come up again,' he said.

He went downstairs again and he got the coal for

the stove, broke the sticks for it, swept up the kitchen, and laid the table for the breakfast. He would have liked to have left all the dirty dishes for Toby, but if he saw them he might go into their room to upbraid them. Everything must look the same as usual.

Then he got his big schoolbag and emptied it out. He discarded all the books, except one, a geography book with coloured maps of all the countries of the world in it. He took the lot of them upstairs again. Derval was in the room, cocooned in clothes, so that she could hardly move. He had to laugh at the sight of her.

'Am I all right?' she asked.

'You are,' he said. 'You will need all those clothes. But we'll take some of them off now, and you go and lie down and sleep, because I don't think we'll get much sleep tonight.'

'I'll never sleep,' she said. 'I know I won't.'

'You'll have to try,' he said.

He took some of the outer garments from her and then helped her into the top bunk. He pulled the blankets over her. She lay down looking at him with one hand under her face.

'Will we have to go across the sea?' she asked.

'We will,' he said.

'In a big boat?' she asked.

'That's right,' he said.

'With money?' she asked. 'I have elevenpence half-penny in my box.'

His heart sank.

'That should do fine,' he said. 'I have some money too. Will you try and go to sleep now, and dream about the sea and the boat?'

'Will the boat be windy?' she asked.

8

He listened. When there was high wind it whistled around this terrace of houses and rattled the windows in their frames.

'No,' he said. 'It won't be windy.'

'You will be with me all the time?' she asked.

'I will,' he said.

'I don't mind so,' she said, and almost at once fell asleep. One second she was wide awake and the next she was fast asleep.

He sat on a chair and thought. What he was going to do seemed utterly impossible. He would have to get himself and his little sister on to a big ship, without money, sail across the Irish Sea and then find a grandmother whose address he did not know. All he knew of her was that dim visit some years ago when he was so small that he could hardly remember a thing about it now. Even when he looked at his diary. He got it out again. It was a small one and he had just learned to write at the time, and he had covered each page with huge letters so there was barely room for more than two or three sentences.

Saturday. We are going on a big boat across the sea.

That was the entry for a full page.

Sunday. We crossed the sea on a big boat.

That was another entry. You stupid boy, he thought, why didn't you give more information? Well, it was the first stage anyhow. He got the tin money box from his own drawer and counted the money in it. Nearly all coppers with a few sixpences.

Seven shillings and tenpence. With Derval's eleven-pence halfpenny, they wouldn't get very far, but it was better than nothing. He thought some more, then, looking at the sleeping girl, he took his air-rifle which was nearly new and his roller skates and he crept out of the room, down into the kitchen and out into the street. It was a long long street of small two-storey houses. It was getting dark. Grey clouds were piling overhead. It would soon rain. He didn't mind that.

Joss lived near the end of the street. He just opened the door and pushed in his head and called, 'Joss!'

'He can't go,' his mother said. 'He hasn't his lessons done.'

'Ah, Mother,' said Joss.

'Only a minute, Mrs Bleaker,' said Finn.

'Mark your minute,' she said, 'or I'll have to beat Joss.'

This was a joke. She wouldn't lay a finger on him.

'I won't be long,' said Joss. He came out.

'Look,' said Finn, holding out the gun and the skates. 'You want those?'

'Boy!' said Joss, eyes gleaming.

'Will you buy them?' Finn asked.

'How much?' asked Joss.

'How much have you got?' Finn asked.

Joss's face fell. 'Not a lot,' he said.

'Go and find out,' said Finn.

Joss went away. Finn kept looking around him, hopping from foot to foot. He felt as if he was being pursued already.

Joss came back. He had money in his hand.

'Ah, it's not enough,' he said. 'Eight and fivepence and a jack knife, that's all.'

10

'Here you are,' said Finn, handing over the gun and the skates.

'But it's not enough,' said Joss.

'It's enough for now,' said Finn, taking the money and the knife. 'I haven't got a knife.'

'It's a real good one,' said Joss. 'It'll do anything. There's even a spike for taking stones out of horses' hooves.'

'That'll be useful,' said Finn, laughing.

'You never know,' said Joss, hurt. 'Are they really mine?'

'They are,' said Finn. 'I must go now.'

'What's your hurry?' said Joss. 'Can't we play with the gun?'

'There are no pellets,' said Finn. 'You'll have to get pellets.'

'Oh,' said Joss. 'All right. I'll see you tomorrow, then.'

'That's the ticket,' said Finn, already moving away.

'What made you do it?' Joss called after him.

'I knew you wanted them,' Finn called back.

'All right, Santa Claus,' said Joss in disbelief, and then started rubbing the butt of the gun with the palm of his hand.

Finn slowed his running. He didn't want to attract attention. Not that there were many people about, but he was already being cautious. He heard questions in his head: When was the last time the boy and girl were seen? Where were they heading for? What were they wearing?

He went to look at Derval first. She was still sleeping.

He started laying out his own clothes. The best way to carry clothes was on your back, he decided. He

11

had two suits, the everyday one with the short pants and the school blazer, and one for Sundays. He had several shirts and jerseys. Some of those he could wear. He had a pair of long jeans. They could go over his shorts. Because he needed the bag for things other than clothes.

He went down to the kitchen again. He looked in the larder. There was cold meat there on the bone. He sliced some of this off, but not too much because Uncle Toby always made meat sandwiches for himself when he came home. He took some butter, and he put on a pot and put eggs into it to hardboil them. He didn't take much bread or all the fruit. He wanted things to look normal if Uncle Toby carried out an inspection. He packed all those things neatly in the bag.

He went upstairs again. It was quite dark in the room now. He knew they would have to be out of the house before Uncle Toby returned, but he didn't want to go until the last minute so that Derval would have plenty of sleep. Otherwise she wouldn't know what was happening to her. Not that she knew much now. He didn't know himself, just that the time had come to get away from Uncle Toby.

He heard the big clock below in the kitchen striking the hours and when it beat out nine o'clock, he started to dress himself, or rather overdress himself. He made sure of the diary that he had it in an inside pocket where he wouldn't lose it. He made sure of the money, and then when he had everything ready he shook Derval.

He had to do a lot of shaking to get her to wake up. When he finally got her awake she looked bewildered and frightened, but then when she recognized him the fright cleared from her face.

12

'We are going to go now, Derval,' he said.

'Oh,' she said.

'We will dress you up again in all your clothes,' he said. 'You look like a small bear.'

She smiled.

He helped her from the bunk, and helped her to put on her extra clothes. She was bulky, but she would need them all.

'All right now?' he asked. She nodded.

'We'll go,' he said.

He put out the light in the room, and they went downstairs. He put her schoolbag over her shoulder and did the same with his. Hers was light, so it would be no great burden on her.

They stood at the kitchen door and he looked at it. One time it was a happy place, he remembered. It was a great pleasure to come home to it. But all the light of laughter was gone out of it since Toby had taken over the power. It was only a place of fear. He was holding Derval's hand. He switched off the light and they went into the street. There was a miserable drizzle falling, but it suited him. They set off to the right. They turned the corner. There was light in the Red Dragon. The windows were misted. He didn't feel safe until they were past it and heading towards the station.

They would have to be hidden in the station before the loaded boat train arrived from London. It was easy to get in when there were no trains. And once all the people were milling about in the early hours of the morning, two children would not be noticed.

They crossed the street towards the station.

Chapter Two

Nobody stopped them going in. It was a very empty place now and badly lighted. But its very emptiness would make them conspicuous. There were very few people about. They could see the ship tied up at the far end, many lights on it, and gangplanks empty. He wondered if they would chance just boldly walking on to it. He decided against this, and they went to a place where an enormous pile of post office bags and other things were heaped, ready to be shifted on to the ship or the returning train.

He went in behind this pile, and they sat down. He would see the train when it pulled in.

'I'm sleepy,' Derval said.

'Shh,' he said, pulling her to lean against him.

He could see the entrance to the station as well. He imagined Uncle Toby running into the station, puffing, looking for them. He knew this couldn't be so. Uncle Toby wouldn't know they were gone until he came down in the morning and found his breakfast wasn't ready, but all the same you couldn't rely on people. Just because he wasn't meant to do a thing, he might just do it. But why would he come to the station? How would he know that they would try and take the ship? He would be more likely to look at the bus station, if he bothered to look at all.

Derval was sleeping.

It was just as well. The train wasn't due for an hour or two yet and it wasn't always on time.

He tried to think of his grandmother. Granny O'Flaherty his mother always called her. His mother was O'Flaherty too, and she had come working in this town across the sea, in a hotel, and she had met Finn's father and his name was Dove and she had married him. These were things he knew for facts. His father was killed in an accident. That was a fact but it was vague. He just remembered feeling a big hole in his chest when his father never came home any more. His mother said he was gone to Heaven, but this didn't satisfy him. Uncle Toby was a fact. His mother married him. Why, he wondered? Just because she was alone and had two young children? Finn couldn't understand grown-ups. If he was his mother he wouldn't marry Uncle Toby for any reason in the world.

He knew his mother had letters from Granny O'Flaherty, but when he went to look for them afterwards Toby had found them and burned them all. Everything belonging to her he had burned. Toby told him why. Because she used me as a convenience, he said. Because she never gave me the things she gave Dove. All she gave me was a shell, Toby said. And she died because she wanted to be with Dove, not me. So I will burn her out of the world. Finn didn't understand all this. Just that Toby was not sober and talked more.

He was startled when he opened his eyes and saw that the train was standing in the station, steam gushing in clouds from under the engine, and that hundreds of people were getting off the train. He couldn't believe he had slept at this important

15

moment. There was a lot of shouting and talking and the clothes of the people getting off the train were creased and wrinkled, and many of them were yawning and rubbing the sleep out of their eyes. He was glad to see that there were many children with their parents, babies in arms, and walking babies, and ones as old as himself and they were all sleepy and some of the babies were crying. They were all walking to the customs shed from where they would get on to the boat.

'Derval! Derval!' he whispered, holding her chin and shaking it. 'Wake up, Derval! Wake up.' It took her a long time to wake and then she rubbed her eyes with her fist. 'All right, now?' he asked.

She nodded, so he caught her hand and stood up, and then walked the few paces from the shelter of the bags into the middle of all the people. This was the way he had seen it and it worked. He and Joss had stolen out many a night and watched all the people getting off the train and on to the boat, and had waited until the boat went off into the bay and watched its lights until it had cleared the end of the pier and was out into the sea. When they did this he had to go home and climb a drainpipe and get into his room by the window. Uncle Toby never knew. So now the knowledge he had acquired then was useful.

Derval didn't quite know what was going on. She seemed to be walking in her sleep. He went right into the mass of people, shuffling with their bags and crying children as they went through the big customs shed. There was no trouble in the customs. He supposed they weren't interested in what people might bring out with them, only in what they might be bringing in. He saw a huge man in front of him,

16

carrying a baby in each arm, his big overcoat swinging open on his broad shoulders. Behind him a lady who was his wife was bringing another child by the hand and carrying a suitcase, and also with them he saw three more bigger children, two boys and a girl all of them carrying suitcases. He squeezed his way through the throng until he was right behind this party.

They all stopped as the crowd going up the gangplank caused a jam. The boys left the bags down. One of them rubbed his wrist.

'Would you like to let me help you with the bag?' Finn asked.

'It has me hand broke,' said the boy.

'I'll help you,' said Finn. 'It has a big handle. The two of us can carry it.'

'Where's your own bag?' the boy asked.

Finn indicated his schoolbag.

'Is that all. You are lucky,' the boy said. 'Are you going to Ireland for a holiday too?'

'That's right,' said Finn.

'We go every year,' the boy said, 'and the bags get heavier.'

They started to move on the gangplank.

'That's because you are all getting bigger,' said Finn, bending and taking hold of the handle of the case. The boy took a hold too and said, 'This is easier.' They followed up the gangplank after the boy's father and mother.

The man in uniform at the top was checking the tickets. He looked back over the man's shoulder at his followers.

'By gob, Peter,' he said, 'every time you come over you have more and more of them.'

17

Peter laughed.

'Somebody has to make up for bachelors like you,' he said. One of the children slipped from his arm and would have fallen if the ticket collector hadn't held the child. The sight of the ticket collector holding the child made Peter laugh, and the people behind him, and while this was happening, Finn went forward with the bag, making the boy follow him, and stepped on the deck of the boat.

'Will you be all right now?' he asked the boy.

'I will,' said the boy, slightly puzzled.

'I have to look for people,' said Finn, moving away holding Derval by the hand.

'We'll see you,' said the boy.

'All right,' said Finn, moving farther and farther away until he saw an open door and stepped into it and walked on the carpet of a lounge. He had to pause here to wipe sweat off his forehead. He went close to the door again and looked out.

The ticket man had handed back the baby. He looked a bit puzzled.

'How many?' he was asking.

'Five,' said Peter. 'I ought to know.'

'I could have sworn there were more,' said the collector.

'Go on, Peter,' said his wife, 'the babies are tired.'

'You don't know how to count,' said Peter.

'Hurry up! Hurry up!' an impatient voice said from the crowd behind them.

'All right,' said the ticket man, dismissing them, but he looked after them once more and scratched his head.

Finn waited to see what Peter and his family would do. They didn't come as far as the door where he was.

They turned right and went another way. He relaxed. He looked around him. People were coming in and taking some of the long seats, putting their coats under their heads and stretching out to sleep. He saw a smaller seat near him so he brought Derval there. He took off the schoolbag and put it down and then took off his coat and put Derval lying down on the seat. She was still very sleepy. She was well wrapped up, but he put his coat over her and she went fast asleep again. Then he went to the far end of the lounge and went out that door. He climbed a ladder to the deck above and looked down at the pier. Big cranes were swinging goods into the hold of the ship. There were men shouting under the arc lights. He could feel the throb of the engines under his feet, as they vibrated the boards of the ship.

He watched the people coming up the gangplanks. They got less and less as he watched.

He was waiting for the gangplanks to be lifted. He felt he wouldn't be safe until this happened. He kept expecting Uncle Toby to come rushing on to the pier, shouting and waving his arms and calling on the ship to stop, stop, until it was searched. He knew this was silly but all the same he was afraid of it. If Uncle Toby did come he would get Derval and go below somewhere. They would find some hole or corner where they could hide.

He found he was biting his thumb. This was something he always did when he was upset. So he stopped biting it. Uncle Toby will not come, he told himself. I have it all worked out. Uncle Toby cannot come.

The big cranes stopped working. He saw the sailors covering the holds and lashing them down.

It seemed hours before at last the gangplanks were

taken away, but they were, and the huge ropes freed from the bollards, but this also was done, and then almost unobtrusively, with some men shouting and bells tinkling, the ship moved away and pointed her bow towards the opening into the bay.

Not until that happened did he leave. He thought of Derval. Suppose she had wakened while he was up there? He went down fast and into the lounge. Derval was sleeping peacefully. So were other people, some of them lying, some of them sitting with their hands folded and their heads nodding. There was no room for him to lie down. He sat and put Derval's feet on his lap, and leaned his head against the back of the seat. He didn't want to go to sleep. Suppose the ticket man came around again? He wanted to be awake for that.

Unfortunately he slept.

The ticket man was halfway down the lounge when he awoke. Some had the tickets in the bands of their hats so that he could check them and not have to awaken them. Others he had to shake awake.

Finn was petrified. For a moment he didn't know what to do. Then he put Derval sitting up, caught hold of the bags and his coat, kept his eye on the ticket man, put the girl's feet on the ground, held her tightly with his free hand and started to back towards the lounge door. Any time the man turned his head he stayed still. Derval was swaying with sleep. He had a job to keep her upright. He thought he would never reach the door unseen, but he did. He got out without a sound. He rested there for a few moments, and then he walked Derval to the far door, the one the ticket man had come in. He kept peering through the sort of porthole of this door, watching the man as he checked to the end of the lounge, and then as he finished and looked around and went out by the other door, Finn went in this one.

He was wet with sweat. Suppose the ticket man had come in the other door instead of this one? He was lucky, he knew. He couldn't afford to go to sleep again. Cautiously he moved down through the sleeping people to the seat they had occupied before. He put Derval lying down again, but he sat upright himself, his ears cocked and his eyes wide open.

Now he suddenly felt cold. Not all the clothes he had on could keep out the cold of the sea air. He put his hands in his pockets. He felt the slight up and down movement of the ship, and the inexorable throb of her engines. The regular beat of the engines was like the beating of a person's heart. It was hypnotic. He was inclined to nod to the rhythm. He shook his head several times, and then finally rose, cautiously looked out and went on deck. He stood where the sheltered part of the deck met the open part and leaned there, the cold air bringing him awake. It wasn't so dark now. There were stars gleaming and where they had come from there was a band of light around the sky. The dawn would soon be here. He could see the white water passing the side of the ship and the slight phosphorescence on top of the broken waves.

What will I do, he wondered, when we reach the other side? He started to panic when he thought of that, but then told himself: What's the use? If we get through we will get through and if we don't I'll think of something.

He remained there until ahead of them he saw the

lights. They seemed to be built-up lights shining from nowhere, but he knew it must be the land, and later he saw the flashing beam of a lighthouse or a light-ship. The sky was brightening and when the lights on the land dimmed and he could make out the shape of the hills that sheltered the houses he went back and woke up Derval.

She looked at him. Her eyes were misted with sleep. He saw fear in them.

'It's me, Derval,' he said. 'It's all right. We are on a ship. Will you wake up properly?'

She nodded her head and sat up.

'We will go out and see,' he said. She nodded and got to her feet. He held her hand and they went out on the deck. It was getting quite bright now. Big sea-gulls were following the ship, calling, zooming and turning effortlessly. He wished that he and Derval were seagulls for the next hour or so, and there would be no trouble ahead of them.

Many people were now coming out of the lounges, stretching themselves and yawning, and gathering up their children and their suitcases. They all moved over to the right side of the ship slowly, so he knew they would be getting off that side and he followed them.

He stayed there in the thickening crowd. There wasn't much talk. People were too tired and it was too early in the morning for talking. He thought about the entry in the diary again.

Mammy said I slept all the time on the ship. When we got off the ship we went on a train. Then we went on another train. This was a train to the west, Mammy said.

22

The little stupid dumb-bell, he thought. Why didn't he say what time or where or what. He remembered only little snatches. He would have been like Derval, he thought. Derval would remember hardly anything of what had happened since they left Uncle Toby's house, so how could this other little boy have remembered? He could have put in a few clues, Finn thought, disgustedly.

He just heard all that happened after that. He couldn't look, there were so many tall people all around him. He didn't want to look anyhow as he felt sheltered and safe among all those people. He wished for a little while that it might always be like this, that he wouldn't have to leave the shelter of their bodies, but the time came when the ship stopped and there was shouting away off, and all of them felt her bumping against the pier, and soon the gangplanks were run up against her and the mass of people started to move.

Now for it, Finn thought, holding Derval's hand tightly.

He followed the crowd. There was no ticket check. They just went down and into this long shed where there were long tables and uniformed men behind the tables opening and examining luggage and then putting a chalk mark on the outside of the cases. Finn just walked straight through the long hall to the swinging doors at the end where another uniformed man was looking at the people and the cases as they went out.

He was a very tall man.

'Hold it,' he said to Finn.

Finn stopped dead.

'No mark on your bags,' the big man said. Finn

23

looked back at the thronged hall. 'Oh, your parents are back there,' he said. 'Well are you carrying smuggled goods in the bag?' He tapped the bulging schoolbag with his finger.

'How about you, little missie?' he asked, bending down to Derval. 'Are you carrying any wine or spirits in the little bag?'

Derval shook her head. She was wearing a hood. Some of her hair was coming out of it. He caught this and gave it a gentle tug. 'All right,' he said. 'Off with you.' He patted her head. Finn realized how useful Derval had been. Most people loved little girls. All the same he got a fright. He wondered if the big man would remember them.

At the bottom of the stairs, the long train was waiting at the platform. They were all separate carriages. You went in one door and there was another the other side. He sat on a seat with Derval. There were a few other people sitting. Then more came in, putting cases up on the racks. It was soon filled, and soon it moved. He didn't look at any of them. He kept his head down. Derval was pressed close to him with her head down too. He didn't know how long the train was running but after a time it stopped and all the people got out of it, and when they were gone he and Derval got down too.

There was a bridge that went from this platform to the other, and there was a long-distance train there. It was going west, he saw. He knew now that this was the train they would have to take. He saw the name of it on a lighted board, but at this stage his amazing luck ran out because when they went up the bridge to get to the other side, there was a fat ticket collector there, and when they went to pass him, he blocked them.

'Where you goin', son?' he asked.

'That train,' said Finn, pointing down.

'You got a ticket?' the man asked.

Finn turned his head, looking behind. It had worked with the big customs man, but it didn't work here.

'You can't travel without a ticket,' the ticket collector said. 'Have you parents?'

Finn would have to answer this directly. It was no good telling lies by looks, which weren't lies.

He knew this man would be unmoved somehow. All he wanted was a ticket.

'You can't travel without tickets,' the man said again.

'Can't our people pay at the other end?' Finn asked.

'What people?' he asked. 'Is there somebody to meet you?'

There wasn't, of course.

'Come on,' said Finn to Derval and they turned back and went down the bridge and from there out of the station. There were a good number of steps leading down to the busy street. There seemed to be an awful lot of houses, an awful lot of shops.

What am I going to do now, Finn wondered? What am I going to do now?

'I'm hungry,' said Derval.

Chapter Three

Life is a chain of evolution. It goes along, nice and orderly until some event breaks the chain, and that leads to further events.

When Uncle Toby found the children gone, he wasn't exactly upset, but he was nonplussed. He searched their room and found that they had taken most of their clothes with them and the schoolbags. He had to go to the kitchen and get his own breakfast. He made a clumsy job of it; the tea overboiled, and the toast burned. He wasn't used to it and he thought of Finn with a certain amount of venom.

As he sat eating his poor breakfast he wondered what people would think. His own conscience was quite clear. He had sacrificed himself for those two children. He had given them all that the heart of children could desire, food and clothes and education (through taxes). He was quite aware that his own behaviour was impeccable.

What would the neighbours think?

This didn't upset him unduly. He thought that the neighbours were quite aware of his worth and would be very sympathetic. Where could they have gone, he wondered. Well, let them stay gone. They would come back again when that boy Finn realized the enormity of his actions. He would come crawling back, begging again for shelter. Uncle Toby was sure of this. Once he had agreed with himself on it, he put the whole thing out of his mind. Let them suffer, he thought. He didn't wash up the dishes. He left them there in the sink. He was sure that when some of the neighbours heard of the plight he had been left in, that they would voluntarily help him, in things like doing a little washing-up and cleaning, and maybe even cooking. They were great people. He would be proud of their charity.

He was a little late getting to work, but that didn't matter either. He was very rarely late and Mr Purdon, he was sure, realized only too well the value of his services.

So he was surprised when he got to the office to find the middle-aged Miss Smith quite fussy.

'You are late, Mr Morgan,' she said. 'Of all mornings to be late when Mr Purdon has been looking for you three times.'

'I was delayed by my cares, Miss Smith,' he said. 'I will go and see Mr Purdon now.'

'Do,' she said, 'right away. It was quite extraordinary the way he has been looking for you.'

'I'm sure we will be able to iron out his troubles,' Uncle Toby said, smugly. He knew he was a good man. It would be difficult to find a better one.

He knocked lightly on the glass door of Mr Purdon's office and went in. Mr Purdon looked at him over his rimless glasses. He was a thin man, very bald with just three or four wisps of hair on the top of his head.

'You're late, Morgan,' he said.

'I'm sorry, Mr Purdon,' Uncle Toby said. 'A slight case of ingratitude. Private matters.'

'An extraordinary thing has happened,' said Mr Purdon.

'What's that?' Uncle Toby asked.

'I had a letter from American solicitors this morning,' he said, 'and if I'm right, it involves you particularly.'

'Me?' said Uncle Toby.

'Yes,' said Purdon. 'The extraordinary thing is that they just picked my name from a reference book in their library, as the solicitor to handle the matter.'

'What's it all about?' Uncle Toby asked.

'You were married to a Mrs Dove, weren't you?'

'Yes,' said Uncle Toby. 'Unfortunately she died.'

'Sad,' said Purdon, in passing. 'But before that her name was O'Flaherty?'

'Yes,' said Uncle Toby.

'And she had two children of the marriage with Dove?' Purdon asked.

'That's right,' said Uncle Toby. 'What is all this about?'

'Well, these American lawyers tell me that an uncle of hers, recently deceased, has left her a large sum of money held in trust for her children, if there are children. In the event of there being no children, or on the death of the children, the trust fund goes to a brother of Mrs Dove in America, a man named Gerald O'Flaherty. Now what do you think of that? Surely she is the lady in question, and the children are the children in question?'

'They are,' said Uncle Toby, sitting down on a chair, 'without any doubt at all. Is the sum big?'

'Invested,' said Mr Purdon, looking at the letter, 'it should provide an income of one thousand pounds a year, sufficient they say for the welfare and full education of the children concerned.'

'But this is impossible,' said Toby. 'It's too much of a coincidence.'

'Strange things happen,' said Purdon, 'but this is not all that strange. Once we have established identity, birth certificates, affidavits, etcetera, as their legal guardian you will be entitled to the interest on the fund. Congratulations, Morgan.'

He was surprised to see the look on Uncle Toby's face. His small eyes were bulging.

'Are you sick?' he asked him.

'The children are gone,' said Uncle Toby.

'Are you mad?' asked Mr Purdon.

'No,' said Uncle Toby. 'When I got up this morning they were gone.'

'Gone where?' Purdon asked.

'I don't know,' said Uncle Toby. 'Just gone.'

'Did you report this to the police?' Purdon asked.

'No,' said Toby, sweating.

'No?' said Purdon, reaching for the phone.

'I was shocked,' said Toby.

'You couldn't have been that shocked,' said Purdon. 'My goodness, Morgan, that's not good. You should have showed anxiety.'

'I was going to see you,' said Uncle Toby desperately, 'to ask your advice.'

'Ah,' said Purdon, looking at him with a cocked eyebrow, 'that was wise. Now I am calling the police. Hello, could I speak to the Inspector? Right. You should have gone straight to the police, Morgan. What came over you? Where could they have gone?'

Uncle Toby grasped at a straw, when he thought of the money involved. 'Maybe their Irish relations snatched them,' he said, 'when they heard about the money.'

'Good gracious,' said Purdon. 'Hello, Inspector. Would you call over here to see me. A matter of some delicacy. The disappearance of two children. Thank you.' He put down the phone. 'Irish relations?'

'Yes,' said Toby. 'She and Dove used to bring them over there on holidays.'

'Ah,' said Purdon. 'If they did this dastardly thing, the children must be declared Wards of Court immediately. You are their legal guardian?'

'Yes,' said Uncle Toby. 'I treated them as if they were my own flesh and blood. Where would they be if I hadn't married their mother and sheltered them all these years?'

'Hum,' said Purdon. 'Apart from that, what evidence have you that the children were taken away?'

'How could they go on their own?' Uncle Toby asked. 'Where would they go on their own? Why would they go on their own?'

'You were kind to them, of course?' said Mr Purdon.

'I sacrificed my whole life for them,' said Uncle Toby. 'Everybody knows that.'

'What ages are they?' Purdon asked.

'The boy is about twelve and the girl about seven,' said Toby.

'Boy should have sense,' said Purdon. 'It's a bit much, all the same, to think of Irish relatives snatching them away.'

'What else could it be?' asked Toby.

The Inspector, a tall well-built man with grey hair, was dubious about the snatching too.

'When was the last time you saw them?' he asked.

Uncle Toby was very sad now. He had a handkerchief in his hand, wiping tears from his eyes. They seemed genuine. He could cry easily.

'At teatime yesterday,' he said.

'You went out after tea?'

'Yes,' said Toby, 'it is my custom to go to the Red Dragon of an evening, drink a few glasses of ale, play a game of darts.'

'So they were in bed when you got home?' the Inspector asked.

'I don't know,' said Toby.

'You didn't tuck them in, see that they were all right?'

'No,' said Toby. 'I don't like to disturb them.'

'Oh,' said the Inspector, 'so they might have been gone when you came in from the Red Dragon?'

'It's possible,' said Uncle Toby.

'That looks like the boat,' said the Inspector. 'Well, I'll make inquiries. I don't like to think of two kids lost like that.'

'You must find them, Inspector,' said Toby. 'They are all I have in life now. We must get them back.'

'Well, we'll get them back all right,' said the Inspector. 'But if they are in Ireland it might be difficult.'

'Nonsense,' said Purdon. 'We'll have them declared Wards of Court here, and if they are over there we can also have them declared Wards of Court.'

The Inspector left them.

'I'm glad you didn't mention about the money, Mr Purdon,' said Toby.

'Why should I?' said Purdon. 'At the moment it's only a sort of speculation. It is a private matter. The important thing now is to find the children.'

'I won't sleep happily again until we have found them,' said Toby.

'Hum,' said Mr Purdon.

The Inspector was later talking on the telephone to an inspector in Dublin.

'I'd say the boat,' he said. 'We found a porter who remembers seeing two kids sleeping on a pile of Her Majesty's Mails. Also one or two inklings that they went on the boat. No clue any other place. Boy has red hair, green eyes, about twelve. Girl about seven, long fair hair, blue eyes. Soft job for you, Mike. Clear it up before teatime. Get them on the next boat. Their stepfather is weeping for them. No, I wouldn't say but that they went on their own. I don't like Mister Tobias Morgan. I think if I was a kid I'd run away from him myself, but that's not our business, is it? You find them and I'll return them. I'll be waiting to hear from you.'

He sat thinking then.

Why would two kids run away from home? They had to have reasons. It had to be the boy of course. He might be a bit of a wild one.

He decided to ask a few questions around the school and the neighbourhood, just to satisfy his curiosity.

Finn didn't know about all this, of course, that all the police machinery of two countries was put into gear to search him out.

He was to find out soon enough.

Chapter Four

They were walking down this narrow street. It was filled with small shops. There were many people walking, and impatient car drivers. Finn stopped at a shop outside of which were crates of empty milk bottles. He thought, then he took one of the empty bottles and walked into the shop with it.

'A pint of milk, please,' he said handing over the bottle.

'Leave the empty outside, son,' the man said to him as he handed over the full bottle. Finn paid. It was the best investment of his limited money, he thought, and young people like Derval had to have milk.

'Thank you,' he said, and went out and left the empty bottle back in the crate. Exchange is no robbery he thought. I will let her drink half the milk now and the rest later on.

'I'm hungry,' she said again.

'We have to find a place to eat,' he said. 'Soon now.'

On the other side of the street, he saw a church. There were steps leading up to it, and huge pillars resting on the steps and supporting the front of the building. There were people coming out of it, blessing themselves from the fonts. He crossed the street and mounted the steps, and they went in through the big doors. It was very quiet in there. There were a few people kneeling down. He looked around. As soon as the door shut all the noises of the street were blocked out. He turned to the left and saw a seat right at the back in a sort of alcove. He went there. It was not a bright place.

'Sit down now,' he whispered, 'and I'll get you the food. Here, you can drink half the milk from the bottle.'

He handed this to her when he had pierced the cap with his fingernail. Derval drank it. Some of it spilled from the sides of her mouth so he said: 'Be careful,' as he wiped it. He opened one of the bags and took out bread and butter and using the knife he got from Joss, he buttered the bread and put some meat between two slices and made thick sandwiches. He gave one of those to her, and the two of them sat there eating the sandwiches. He was surprised to find how hungry he was himself, and how tasty the sandwich was.

Where do I go now, he wondered?

By this time, Uncle Toby would know that they were gone, and he was afraid it wouldn't be hard for him to guess *where* they had gone. His heart raced when he thought of Uncle Toby chasing after them. This was only his imagination, because there was no real reason why Uncle Toby should chase after them.

Since they couldn't get on the train, they would somehow have to follow the train. If he could find the road that went the same way as the railway, they could walk, or get lifts. He could think of a story that wasn't a lie, maybe, and if they were lucky they could get a lift the whole way.

He knew there was a road running near the railway. He remembered that. He remembered pointing out to his mother the place where there was a road with cars on it, and a canal with a barge on it, and they in the train, and for a minute or two those three lines were side by side. So that would be what they would have to do. That had to be the next thing. He recalled the entry in the diary:

We got off the train, and then we got into a big bus. It was a green bus. It rattled.

So if they got to the place where the train stopped they would see the right bus. He hoped he might be able to remember.

He tidied up and they left the church. He stood on the steps outside. The sun was shining. It was shining in their faces. Now, then, he thought, the sun rises in the east and sets in the west. If it came up out of the sea this side of the country, it would go into the sea the other side. That would be west. Taking a rough line, then, he continued on up the long street. It was a long one. Then there was a place where this street crossed another broad street. It took them ages to get across. From here the next wide street climbed. Each side of the street there were tall brick houses, with steps up to the front doors. There was not as much traffic here, but there seemed to be an awful lot of children, screaming and shouting, and suddenly from a group farther up, a big rubber ball came through the air and hit Derval on the side of the head, and knocked her down.

Finn picked her up from the ground. There was a round dirty mark on her face where the ball had hit her. She couldn't make up her mind whether to cry or not and then she decided not to.

He looked around and found that they were

surrounded by a group of boys. One of them had picked up the ball, tucked it under his arm and now approached Finn with a most belligerent countenance. He had ginger-coloured hair standing up in spikes. He pushed his face close to Finn's and said:

'Do you want a fight?'

Finn considered this.

'No,' he said, 'why would I want to fight?'

'The ball hit your little sister,' said the boy.

'It didn't kill her,' said Finn.

'I'd fight if a ball hit my little sister,' he said.

'Did you mean the ball to hit my sister?' Finn said.

'No,' said the boy, 'why would we do a thing like that?'

'If you didn't mean to hit her it was an accident,' said Finn.

'That's right,' said the boy.

'Why should we fight over an accident, so?' Finn said.

The boy creased his nose thinking over this, then he smiled, showing white pointed teeth. 'That's right,' he said. He held out his hand. 'Shake,' he said. 'I'm Poll. This is Trumpet, Finbar, Totem, Pudger, Casey, Mini, Gussie, Fleet and Percy.'

'I'm Finn,' said he. 'Hello, fellas.'

'Hello,' they said, looking at him curiously.

'Where did you get the funny accent?' Poll asked.

'I was going to ask you the same thing,' said Finn.

'My accent isn't funny,' said Poll. 'Yours is and you're not a culchie.'

'What's a culchie?' Finn asked.

'Ah, that's a fella from the country,' said Poll. 'Where are you from?'

'Over the sea,' said Finn.

'I knew you weren't a culchie,' said Poll. 'What are you doing up our side?'

'We're going out to the west,' said Finn, pointing towards the sun.

'Will you play football?' Poll asked.

'I don't mind,' said Finn, 'if you tell me how to go west afterwards.'

'We will,' said Poll. 'We are a man short. Now we'll be evens. Come on. Can we use your little sister?'

'She can't play football,' said Finn.

'Nah, not that,' said Poll. 'Come on. You'll see.'

They ran out in the broad street. There wasn't a lot of traffic on it. They were playing on the road near a railings that enclosed a park with a lot of grass inside it.

'Why don't you play in the park?' Finn asked.

'Ah, that's private,' said Poll. 'The gates is locked. They don't like young people in there. Now look, we want your sister for a goalpost. Will she stand over there?'

Finn looked. They had three little girls. They were sitting on the boys' coats, two at the far end and one near here.

'Come on, Derval,' he said taking her by the hand. There was a small girl sitting on coats. She was dark. Her hair was cut in a fringe.

'That's my sister, Fiona,' said Poll. 'This is Finn's sister,' he said to her. She just put a finger in her mouth.

Finn stripped off some of his double clothes. He put them on the ground. 'Sit there now, Derval,' he said. 'You are a goalpost.' Derval sat down obediently and looked at the other goalpost. They were both shy.

'Now we can play,' said Poll.

Finn thought it was a very useful thing to make goalposts out of little sisters.

He enjoyed the game of football. They had to stop now and again to let a car or a lorry pass. Some of the lorry drivers were angry and spoke freely about kids playing football on the public streets, but they were answered vigorously by the boys, by word of mouth and various rude signs.

Once they had to flee into a side lane, gathering up the goalposts and the clothes when somebody saw a policeman coming. But it gave them a rest from the play, added a touch of drama to the game, and when the policeman had gone they went back again to the game with added vigour.

Finn enjoyed it all very much. It made him forget his troubles. He was sorry when a woman leaned out of a window near the top of the tall house and screamed, 'Poll! Poll! Come in for your dinner! Your dinner is ready.'

'Aw, Mother,' shouted Poll.

'If ye don't come in I'll go down for ye!' she called and pulling in from the window, banged it shut.

'Aw,' said Poll. 'We'll have to go in for the old dinner.'

'That's fine,' said Finn. 'We'll be on our way.'

'Where'll you get your dinner?' Poll asked

'We have food in the bags,' said Finn.

'That's not a dinner,' said Poll. 'Come on in with us and have dinner. She won't mind.'

'Who's she?' asked Finn.

'My mother of course,' said Poll. 'Arrah, come on, you'll see. Wouldn't the little sister be better with a dinner in her?'

'She would, I suppose,' said Finn.

'Come on so,' said Poll. 'Can't ye go west afterwards?'

Finn thought it over. He liked the boys. He wouldn't mind seeing a bit more of Poll, and besides it would postpone his decision.

'All right,' he said.

He gathered his clothes and carried them on his arm with the bags and took Derval's hand and followed the boys to the stone steps that led up to the tall house. There was a long row of these tall houses, all built of brick.

'Where are we going?' Derval asked.

'We are going in with the boys to have dinner,' he said.

'When will we be going to Granny?' she asked.

'Soon,' said Finn, his heart sinking.

There was a hall. It was fairly dirty. There were several crocks of prams in the hall. They climbed a stairs. The boards of the stairs were worn from the feet of people. They climbed one flight and there was another hall, with prams and other things in it. They climbed another flight, and came to another hall. This wasn't as cluttered and the things in it were tidy. There was a great smell of cooking. They lost some of the boys on the way, but on this hall-landing there were five of them left with the girl Fiona.

'Here we are,' said Poll, opening a door.

'Do these all belong to you?' Finn asked.

'That's right,' said Poll, counting them off as they went in: 'Trumpet, Finbar, Totem, Pudger, Mini and Fiona.'

'Are they all your brothers?' Finn asked.

'Sure they are,' said Poll. 'It's a pity we haven't

more or we'd have a football team when they grow up, my father says. Hello, Mother,' he said then as they went in the door. 'I brought Finn and his little sister. They have no place to get their dinner.'

It was a big room with a high ceiling. There was a sort of wooden army table in the centre. The young ones were already sitting around it. The woman who had screamed out the window turned from the range. Her face looked hot. There was some of her hair falling over her cheek and she brushed it back. She was a young woman. She had frowns on her forehead.

'Oh, Poll,' she said, 'where'll we put them? Why didn't you tell me? I'd have put more in the pot.'

'We'll go away again, ma'am,' said Finn. 'We wouldn't upset you.'

'You will not go away again,' she said coming over to them, wiping her hands on her apron. 'You'll sit down at the table. We can stretch what's in the pot. You're welcome,' shaking hands with him and putting her hand on Derval's head. 'If only Poll had told me.'

'But it only happened now,' said Poll. 'I didn't know until this minute.'

'All right, Poll,' she said. 'Push over on the bench,' she said to the others. 'Sit down, Finn.' She lifted Derval and put her sitting beside Fiona. 'You're right welcome.'

She went to the range and brought back a pot of stew. She ladled this out to them into the soup plates that were set at the table. The boys could hardly wait for it to be on their plates before they started to scoop it into their mouths. It was very good stew, Finn thought, as he tasted it.

Poll's mother didn't sit down and eat at all. She was

40

after her children all the time. 'Trumpet, don't be eat-ing like a savage! Fiona, keep the napkin around your neck. Look what you are doing to your dress. Pudger, will you mind Mini. Look at the way he's slopping.' He felt good to be in the middle of a family like this.

They had finished the stew and were eating bread and jam when the door opened and a red-haired man came in, taking bicycle clips from his trousers.

As soon as he got into the room, he shouted, 'Squad! Rise! Attenshun.'

The young ones rose from their places and stood up stiffly, even Fiona, who stuck out her tummy. They had formed up in a line, laughing and trying not to laugh, and the man went down the line inspecting them, saying, 'Shoulders up, stomachs in. Where's your button? Six days' kitchen police, my lad. All right back to rations. Hold it!' when he saw Finn and Derval. 'What's this? How did I get two more chil-dren since this morning? Can you explain this, Mary?' to his wife who was putting his dinner on to a plate.

'Poll brought them in,' she said.

'This is Finn, Daddy,' said Poll, 'and his sister Derval.'

'It's a strange thing,' he said, holding out his hand to Finn, 'that you are the first red-headed son in the family, just like me. Hello, Derval. How are you?'

'Here's your dinner, Tom,' his wife said. 'Can't you eat it first and talk afterwards.'

'Finn came from over the sea,' said Poll. 'We were playing football.'

'Did you swim across, Finn?' Tom asked.

'No,' said Poll, 'they came on the boat.'

'Your mother and father?' Tom asked.

41

Finn looked at him. Tom had a lot of laugh wrinkles on his face. He was a kind man, Finn thought. His children liked him. They were all around him now, hanging on to him. Also he had shrewd eyes, even if they were laughing. Finn wondered what tale to tell him.

'We were separated,' he said.

'A big boy like you got lost?' Tom asked.

They were very kind, Finn thought.

'My father and mother are dead,' he said.

'Oh,' said Tom. 'How were you wandering around the streets?'

'Well, we got off the boat,' said Finn, 'and we didn't have enough money to go any farther.'

'Where's farther?' Tom asked.

'We are going to Granny,' said Derval.

'You are, love,' he said. 'That's nice. No more talk now until we finish the grub.' He patted Derval's head and looked now and again at Finn. His look didn't make Finn feel uneasy.

Finally he rubbed his mouth and said, 'All right, you kids, off and play. I'll see ye again.'

'Can't I stay?' Poll asked.

'No,' said Tom. 'Scoot, Poll, and we'll see you again. Off with ye now. Into the ranks, shoulder arms, quick march.'

He got them out this way and closed the door after them.

'I used to be in the Army,' he said to Finn, as if his behaviour demanded an explanation. He lifted Derval in his arms and sat down on a chair seating her on his knee. 'Well, Derval,' he said to her, 'so you are going to Granny.'

'Yes,' she said. 'Granny is nice.'

'You ran away from home, Finn?' he asked.

'We ran away,' said Finn.

'Oh,' said Tom looking at him. For a boy he had a very determined chin, Tom thought. 'Wasn't the place you ran away from home?'

'Only Uncle Toby,' said Finn.

'Who is Uncle Toby?' Tom asked.

'He married my mother when Father died,' said Finn. 'He used to be a lodger.'

His face was completely closed, Tom saw. That was the story of Uncle Toby.

'And where's your granny?' he asked.

'Somewhere in the west,' said Finn. 'When we go to the station and we see the buses I will know where she is.'

'You know that Uncle Toby is your guardian and he can get you back?' Tom asked

'If he gets me back,' said Finn, 'we will just go away again.'

'Uncle Toby beat Finn,' said Derval.

'Quiet, Derval,' said Finn.

'I see,' said Tom. Derval was holding his hand quite confidently. 'You know what will happen? The police over there will ring the police over here, and they'll pick you up and send you back.'

'Why would they do that?' Finn asked. 'Uncle Toby doesn't care for us.'

Tom looked at Mary. Her eyes were sad.

'He'll have to,' said Tom. 'The neighbours will report it. The police will have to look for you.'

'We are going to Granny,' said Finn with determination.

Tom thought over it, one of his fingers playing with Derval's hair.

43

'You are entitled to a shot for freedom,' he said, 'but you have a long way to go. It was as well you didn't get on the train.'

'Why?' Finn asked.

'Trains always go to known destinations. They could have plucked you from the train at any of the stations. Also it would be as well for you to get out of this city fast. You come with me now, and I'll put you on the right road.' He was standing.

'Tom,' said Mary, 'couldn't they stay with us for a while? He can't be going miles with the little girl.'

'He's come a long way with her so far,' said Tom. 'Maybe he'll go the distance. He's entitled to try. How is the grub situation? Show me your bags.'

He inspected the bags.

'Here, Mary,' he said, 'put in a few more bits and pieces. I have to get back to work. You will come with me. I know a man who always travels west on a Friday, I have a feeling you ought to go before they catch up with you.'

'Are you doing the right thing, Tom?' Mary asked.

'What do you want me to do?' he asked. 'Keep them here and call the police?'

She thought over this and then started making sandwiches.

She kissed Derval before they left, looking at her sadly.

They went down the stairs.

In the bottom hall, Tom said, 'Just follow me. I'll have the bicycle but I won't ride it. I'll walk with it. Just keep near me.'

He went out and took the bicycle and when he moved to the street, wheeling it, they followed him. The children stood on the street with their hands

44

behind their backs looking at them. Poll waved a hand, and Finn waved back at him, but all the time he kept his eyes glued on the figure of Tom.

Now they were hardly out of this street when a tall grey-haired man with no hat on him and a raincoat came into this street. His name was Michael and he was a detective. He had been talking to the people at the boat and the people in the train and he had talked to a ticket collector who remembered two children with no tickets, a red-haired boy and a little girl. He had found a shop where a boy had bought a bottle of milk. He had seen crumbs in a church, and he had walked up this street by chance and a certain amount of acumen.

He stopped and saw the children playing.

He raised a hand and called to the biggest child.

'Hey, son,' he said. 'Come here a minute.'

'Is it me?' Poll asked.

'Yes,' said Michael, 'I just want to talk to you.'

After hesitating, Poll walked over towards him.

45

Chapter Five

The detective Michael was talking on the telephone to the Inspector across the sea.

'What kind of a detective are you at all?' the Inspector asked. 'Here's two kids in a small country and you couldn't catch them.'

Michael said, 'That red-haired kid is no gom. He got on that boat under your noses, crossed, and got off before you gave us notice. I can tell for sure there was no conspiracy and no kidnapping. The children were on their own.'

'I didn't think it likely that they were taken,' said the Inspector. 'Uncle Toby doesn't believe it now either.'

'What's he like?' Michael asked.

'The funny thing is that I think he's sincere,' said the Inspector. 'He's really crying about the kids. You wouldn't think there was any reason. He seems definitely upset. The neighbours I have spoken to speak well of him. A jolly man, they say. There seems to be no reason for him to be upset unless he has a genuine feeling for them.'

'Why did they run away from him, so?' Michael asked.

'The boy Finn,' said the Inspector. 'He's the leader type. A good boy, they say, bright in school. Uncle Toby says it's the Irish in him that makes him embark on an adventure like this. You better find him fast or you'll have Uncle Toby down on your neck.'

'Oh, no,' said Michael.

'Oh, yes,' said the Inspector. 'He's talking of going over to look for them himself, appealing to the Press as well.'

'Oh, no,' said Michael.

'Oh, yes,' said the Inspector. 'You have loads of trouble coming up, boy, unless you find those kids and send them back fast. What trace of them have you?'

'I followed their trail off the boat, on to the train to the station, and then as he tried to bluff himself on to the train to the west. It's a pity they didn't let him on and we'd know where they were and could have caught them. Then they ate a meal in a church and after that I'm sure they played football in a street. I questioned a lot of kids, and I'm positive they were with them, because all the kids in a body deny that they were. I don't think they are being sheltered in the street. I have a feeling that they have left the street and are now miles away, but I don't know how or in what direction. As soon as the kids are off the streets and in bed I'll talk to some of the grown-up people. They might have seen something. Then we'll get moving.'

'You'd better,' said the Inspector, 'or not only will you have Uncle Toby on your back, you'll have all the newspapers as well.'

'But why is it so important?' Michael asked. 'Two kids run away from home to go to their granny. What's big about that?'

'Uncle Toby wants the kids back,' said the Inspector.

'There's something else,' Michael insisted.

'Not as far as we know,' said the Inspector.

'There has to be,' said Michael, 'or it doesn't make sense.'

'You are not paid to be introspective,' said the Inspector. 'You just get on with it, Mike.'

'Where does the granny actually live?' Michael asked. 'If that's where they are going, we could sit back and wait for them there.'

'Don't,' said the Inspector. 'They are being declared Wards of Court here and also over with you. Suppose they do get to the granny and she determines to hold on to them, boy, you are going to be in trouble then. Uncle Toby doesn't know where the granny lives. Somewhere in the west.'

'That's a wide area,' said Michael. 'It doesn't matter. We'll have them tomorrow and on their way home before there is any fuss.'

'You'd better,' said the Inspector.

'I wish I'd never heard of them,' said Michael.

'Better still,' said the Inspector, 'I bet you wish you knew where they were.'

Michael didn't answer him.

At that time they were in the front of a very old rickety van, avoiding the steel springs that were protruding from the torn upholstery and laughing away at Mickser, a fat man in a bowler hat, wearing a moustache, who was singing a song that he made up himself as he went along. Finn thought he was jolly, real jolly, not like Uncle Toby.

Chapter Six

They had followed Tom a long way, through various streets and side alleys until they came to this place of one-storey houses, which ended in a cul-de-sac. Here Tom left his bicycle against one of the houses near a black gate of wood that was very crooked and broken.

He made a sign to them and went in here.

They waited for him. There wasn't much activity in the street, just one small brown dog that came up and sniffed at them, while Derval circled Finn as he did so, but his interest soon waned and he went back and lay on the pavement in the afternoon sun.

Then Tom came out and signalled them.

'We're in luck,' he said. 'Mickser is just about to set out. Another half an hour and we would have missed him.'

They followed him into the yard. It was a very untidy place. It was filled with scrap iron and old bedsteads, and broken machinery and rusted pipes, old gas cookers, thick radiators, with just enough room for an old van. There was an old tarred shed too, that seemed to have been put together from junk. The windows were all of different sizes, and when Mickser came out of here, Finn noticed he had twinkling eyes, so he took to him almost straight away.

'You want to go away on your holidays,' he said,

coming to them. 'Tom told me of ye. I will be travelling west soon. Won't I be delighted to have ye as passengers? Hello, little miss.' He bent down to shake hands with Derval. She looked at him for a little time before she held out her hand. 'I'm not used to females travelling with me,' he told her, 'but we'll put a bit of satin on the seat for you, eh? How would you like to sit on satin?'

Derval laughed.

'There,' he said, 'you'll travel like a queen.'

'Finn,' said Tom, 'I have a big family as you saw. It's little I can afford after feeding them, but here's this to see you on your way.'

He held out a ten-shilling note. Finn backed away from it.

'No, no!' he said. 'You mustn't do that. We have money. I sold things. Now that Mister Mickser is taking us, I won't need even what I have.'

Tom put the money into Finn's pocket.

'You never know,' he said.

'You have been very kind to us,' said Finn. 'Why is this?'

Tom was nonplussed.

'Well,' he said, 'you have made a brave effort to do something. It must mean a lot to you. Why wouldn't I help you? I help you and you will remember it, and some time when you are big you will help somebody else in trouble. You see this. It is a sort of a circle that will never end.'

'I won't forget,' said Finn.

'I better get back to work,' said Tom. 'Mickser will see ye on the way. If you are ever back in the city, you know where to find us.'

He didn't say goodbye to them. He just ruffled

Derval's hair and then went out without looking back.

Finn looked after him.

'That's a good man,' said Mickser. 'He has only one fault. He likes children. Now I have no use at all for children. They are nothing but great trouble. Here, missie, look what I found in my pocket.'

With an air of great surprise he took a block of chocolate covered with purple paper from his pocket and handed it to Derval. She laughed and took it. He handed another one to Finn.

'Why are we laying about here?' he asked then. 'Shouldn't we be on the road? We have to be fifty miles away before the night.' He lifted Derval into the front of the van. 'You close the gate when I back out,' he said to Finn, and climbed in beside the girl. Finn went back to the old gate.

He heard Mickser trying to start the engine. It turned over many times before it caught and then it belched very black smoke from the exhaust, backfired, caught and settled down to a loud throb. Then Mickser looked out through the window at the back of the van. It wasn't really a window as there was no glass in it, just a square hole cut out of the timber.

The van was open in the back with low sides, and green canvas on the floor of it, otherwise it was empty. It came backing erratically out of the yard, and when it had passed, Finn tried to close the black gate. This was difficult as it was sagging on its hinges, but he pulled it closed with a great effort. There was no way to lock it, but Finn didn't think there was anything in the yard that would be worth stealing.

'Come on,' Mickser called, 'that's enough. I put a

curse on the place. Anyone that goes near the place'll turn into rusty iron. Climb aboard, and let us be away.'

Finn laughed and got into the van. Although Derval was small and he didn't take up much room himself, Mickser was very spread and the van was small, so they were well crowded. The van behaved well as long as it got a straight run, but when they came into the heavy traffic and it had to stop at traffic lights, Mickser found it hard to get it going again, and the drivers behind him would start hooting impatiently while he was trying. He would put his head out of the window then, and shout things at them, about who did they think they were, and did they think they owned the city and nobody had a right to stall in it except themselves.

This happened twice. Finn kept his eye on the policemen who watched this. Once one of them made a move to come over to Mickser, but fortunately the van got going before he was near them, and Finn found himself shrinking back against the seat. He was afraid now of the sight of the uniform. Before, he hadn't even thought of policemen as people to avoid.

It seemed ages to him until they were clear of most of the traffic and bowling at about twenty miles an hour if you could believe the speedometer that had no glass in front of the pointing-hand. It was a long dual carriageway road they were on and there was plenty of room for the other cars and lorries to roar past them.

'Look at them,' Mickser would say. 'You'd think all belonging to them were dead and they were late for the funeral. On with ye!' he'd shout, 'Kill yerselves. That's right.' Then he would say to Derval,

'All right, Queenie, as a distinguished foreigner, what do you think of our country?'

'The fields are green,' said Derval, because they were well out into the country now.

'Ah,' said Mickser, 'you pity the poor creatures that live out here. Nothing but pigs and cattle and sheep and the big sky, and not a pub to be seen within twenty miles. God help them. If they didn't see civilized persons like ourselves once in a while they'd pass out.'

Finn noticed that Mickser didn't ask them one question about themselves. He must have wondered what they were up to, where they were going or trying to go, what their journey was all about, but he kept silent.

They stopped once at a place beside the road where there was a garage with petrol pumps and an inn.

He made the man put in a couple of gallons of petrol, and then saying to them, 'I won't be long,' he went into the inn.

The attendant put his head in the window and looked at them.

'Are ye Mickser's children?' he asked. 'It's the first time I ever saw him with children.'

'No,' said Finn. 'He's giving us a lift.'

'I thought he might be trading ye in for old lead pipe,' he said grinning. 'Mickser would trade in his mother for a bit of copper.'

'He's a nice man,' said Finn, frowning at the man.

'Indeed he is,' he said. 'I'm only joking. The road wouldn't be the same without Mickser travelling it.'

'You mind your own business, Ned,' said Mickser behind him. 'Your nose'll grow so long you'll end up like an elephant. Here, Queenie,' he said, 'I brought you some lemonade.' He handed in a bottle of lemonade with a straw in it. He had another one for Finn. He also gave them two big round biscuits with currants baked into them. 'Wallop those, I won't be long.' He went back into the inn again.

It was nice lemonade. It was full of fizz. The attendant wandered away from them. The biscuits were hard and crunchy. When Mickser came back he was wiping his mouth. He rubbed the ends of his moustache with a forefinger.

'You have to bring them the news of civilization,' he said as he set off again. 'They might as well be living in the horse age.'

'Haven't they radio and television?' Finn asked.

'Oh, yes,' said Mickser, 'but how can they understand what they hear and see if there isn't someone like me to sort of be an interpreter for them?'

'You are very kind,' said Finn.

Mickser looked at him sharply and laughed.

'I tell them great tales from the city,' he said. 'I hope they believe me.'

It was almost dusk when they came up this hill and saw the town below them. Some lights were lit.

'We have to stop here for awhile, said Mickser. 'I have a bit of work to do. Then we'll pull out of the town and we'll make a nice bed in the van under a tree by the river, and tomorrow we'll head off west. Does this suit you, young Finn?'

'It sounds marvellous,' said Finn, wondering at how easily they were being transported to their destination, with almost no effort on his part at all. All he had done was get them on the boat and across the sea, and now they were on their way to the end of the road just as if somebody had spread a magic carpet for them, if you could think of Mickser's van as a magic carpet.

He laughed at this thought.

'Keep laughing,' said Mickser. 'Nobody pays you for crying unless you are working in an onion factory.'

They coasted down the hill to the town. There was a kind-looking red colour in the sky.

Chapter Seven

It seemed to be a town of one main street with several branches off it. The tallest building in it would be of three storeys. The others were two-storey or single-storey houses, most of them turned into shops of various kinds. Cars and lorries were parked along the length of it and it was hard to get through. There were no traffic lights and people seemed to be just walking aimlessly across the street always in danger of being knocked down.

Mickser drove almost the full length of the street before he turned left into a side street, and about halfway down that he turned right into a sort of narrow alleyway, and after that turned left again, until he ended up outside a place where there was a black gate similar to his own at home in the city. He honked his horn here, and after a while, a thin bald man opened the gate and looked out at them. He peered for a while, and then he started to open the gate.

'Back in,' he called, so Mickser proceeded with the complicated backing in that narrow way, with a lot of shouting and encouragement from the bald man. Finally he had the van backed in and he said to Finn, 'I won't be long now. I just have to put some stuff in the van and we can be on our way.' He looked at Derval. She was sleepy. She was leaning against Finn's chest. He had his arm around her. 'Were you right to bring a young one like that on a trip like this?' he asked. He wasn't laughing. Finn felt his own heart dropping.

'I had to,' he said. 'I just had to.'

'As long as you know what you are doing,' said Mickser. 'I won't be long.'

He left Finn with his thoughts. They were a bit black now as he felt the gentle breathing of his sister on his chin. It was a chance he had taken. It had turned out well so far, and it would turn out better tomorrow. By then they should be within hailing distance of their granny. He would find her somehow, and then she would take over Derval. He comforted himself with this thought.

He heard the sounds as something heavy was put on the van behind them. He didn't know what it was. Even if he had he wouldn't have been much enlightened anyhow. It was long sheets of copper rolled up like paper. They were heavy. Even Mickser was grunting as he lifted each roll into the back of the van. There were thirty of them altogether, and they made the van sag a little on its springs. Finally they were all loaded, and Mickser put his hand into his inside pocket and took out a bundle of notes and he counted them into the bald man's hand.

'All right,' he said.

'Fine,' said the bald man. 'It'll be a while again before I send you a note. This was a close one.'

'They know nothing?' Mickser asked.

'No,' said the bald man. 'Not a smell of them.'

'Good,' said Mickser.

He climbed into the van again.

'That's it,' he said. 'Now we can be on our way.'

He started the engine and they waited for the bald man to open the gate.

He did this and the van drove into the roadway, and turned right.

As it did so, they heard Mickser exclaiming. They had the lights of the van shining now and in the light they could see the uniform of policemen coming down the street. There were two of them and there was purpose in their approach. They were walking in the centre of the roadway.

'Oh,' said Mickser. He stopped the van and put her into reverse gear and roared backwards, his head out of the window.

As he passed the bald man's gate, they could see policemen going in there too. One of them shouted and started to run towards the van, Mickser kept reversing. Finn was watching all this and his stomach was tight. Suddenly there was a lot of sweat on Mickser's face.

He stopped reversing and drove the van into another lane. It was very narrow. He turned left and proceeded and turned right, and then stopped.

'Get out, Finn, fast. I'm nicked. They were watching the place. I don't want them to see you. Slip out and hide in a doorway.' Finn had already shaken Derval awake. 'I'm sorry, Queenie,' he said to the child, rubbing a finger on her soft cheek.

Finn lifted her down, along with the bundle of their clothes and the bags. He closed the door.

'Walk out of the town the west way,' said Mickser urgently. 'The first bridge you come to about a mile from the town go down under it. It's a shelter. If I don't come by around twelve tomorrow, don't wait. Keep going.'

He started the van again and roared away.

Finn looked desperately for a doorway.

There was one near him. It was a two-storey house that was decayed. There was a sagging wooden door on it. Holding Derval's hand he went in there. There was a pile of rubble where the roof and upper floor had collapsed. He pulled in here with his back to the wall. He listened. He heard the sound of running footsteps, calling voices. When they passed, he still stood holding Derval in front of him. It was as well they waited. Soon he heard the sound of the van coming back. It was going slowly. As it passed the doorway he heard a man laughing. He heard him speaking. He had to speak loudly over the sound of the engine.

'Oh, you walked into that one, Mickser,' he heard him say. Mickser didn't say anything at all.

Finn didn't relax until he could hear no further sound. Then he came out from the doorway and looked. The lane was dark, but there was still light enough in the sky to see that it was empty. He thought that the police must have had all the area cordoned off to catch Mickser at whatever he was up to. Now that they had him, it should be free.

'Come on, Derval,' he said.

They came into the lane.

If he went back the way to get into the main street, they might run into them again, so he went right, and then he saw a narrow way that ran right again. He followed this way. When he came to the end of it he thought he saw light ahead of him and he cautiously turned to his right and saw the street-lights in front. He walked down here and found himself on the main street.

It was near closing-time. Some of the shops were shut. Many of the cars had left their parked positions.

People were hurrying. The street-lights were not very bright. He looked up and down the street and when he saw the sunset sky to his left he turned and walked that way.

Some people looked at them as they passed on the pavement, but not many, and they were just casual looks. All the same his heart was beating fast. He expected a hand to fall on his shoulder and a voice to say, 'Are you Finn?' But it didn't happen. They kept walking. The line of shops ended, and then there were houses, and then a long wall on one side whitewashed, and then a church with railings around it, and then an open field and another open field, and soon they were walking a road where the pavement had ended. Each side of the road there were hedges and tall trees. In fact the trees had closed in over their heads, but there was still an odd light on a fence post. But even those ended when the trees ended, and they were walking by the hedges, pulling in close to one as a car with its blinding lights came towards them or behind them.

Then the hedges ended and the sides of the road had concrete posts with wire strung from them, and about fifty yards away he saw the remaining light gleaming on the waters of a river.

'Where are we going, Finn?' Derval asked. She was clutching his hand tightly. She was frightened. No wonder since he was frightened himself.

'We won't be long now,' he said, because he saw the bridge ahead of him. He stopped on the bridge. It was a stone bridge. He looked over. It had three arches. It was a fairly wide river. He looked at the stone walls near him as they joined the bridge. They were broken down, presumably by children who wanted to play near the river.

60

'Down here,' he said to Derval.

They climbed over the wall and into the short grass of the field. He came to the first arch of the bridge. The river was only half flowing through this arch. On the left supporting the arch there was an abutment, a long one, low and about two feet wide. The ground under it was dry too, so they sat here. There was no danger of the river rising.

'Are you hungry?' he asked her.

'I am,' she said. 'Where are we, Finn?'

'We are sitting on a nice place under a bridge,' he said. 'We will be able to make a nice bed here, and tomorrow we'll find Granny.'

'Oh, good,' said Derval.

'Start on this,' he said, handing her the bar of chocolate that Mickser had given him. Then he opened the bag and got out the bread and butter. They still had some milk in the bottle but he saw that it had gone sour, so he walked the short distance to the water of the river which was only about a foot deep and seemed clean as it ran over gravel, and he washed out the bottle and filled it with water and brought it back.

Fortunately Derval was getting sleepy, so when she had eaten enough he made a bed from their spare clothes and wrapped her well, and with one of the bags for a pillow, she fell asleep and he was grateful for this. He leaned against the arch, his feet on the abutment and he munched away at the bread and drank water from the bottle, and he reflected that he was now on his own. He didn't think that Mickser would turn up again, so they would have to find their own way to the west. He didn't know how they were going to do this, but he knew they were going to do

61

it, and maybe it was as well he was on his own. He tucked his hands into the sleeves of his jacket and hunched himself up and tried to sleep. He smelled cattle. They would come in here for shelter, he thought, from the rain and the wind. He heard nothing else, just the sibilant hissing of the water as it met and was divided by the buttress of the arches. In the distance a dog was barking.

That was the last thing he heard until he was awakened, startled by the sound of a voice calling his name, 'Finn! Finn!'

Chapter Eight

It took him quite a time to come to full awareness. The voice calling him seemed like the voice in a dream, his father or his mother. He looked around him. He was cold. He was in such a strange place, under a stone arch, with the sound of a river, and the voice still calling softly, 'Finn! Finn!'

He got to his feet. He had to hobble around a bit because there were pins and needles in his right leg. Derval was still sleeping. He went to her and put his hand on her mouth and called, 'Derval, wake up.'

He saw her eyes opening. There was fright in them, and then the fright went out of them when she saw Finn. He took his hand away. 'Be ready to go fast,' he said, 'in case we have to. There is somebody calling me.'

He went cautiously out of the arch and looked up. He was much relieved to see the fat moustached face of Mickser looking down at him.

'Don't come up,' said Mickser. 'They still have their eye on me.'

'Will we be able to go on?' Finn asked.

'No,' said Mickser sadly. 'That's why I walked out here. I was never made for walking. They kept my van. It's evidence.'

'What happened?' Finn asked.

'Imagine,' said Mickser. 'That fellow I bought the

63

copper from had nicked it from a building site. They were waiting for him to sell it. I bought it.'

'You didn't know it was stolen?' Finn asked.

'Would a man like me do a thing like that?' Mickser asked. Finn thought he would, but didn't like to say so.

'Now they'll persecute me,' said Mickser. 'I'll have to thumb home. Is there no law in the land to protect innocent people like me I asked them?'

'And what did they say?' Finn asked.

'They said that fortunately there wasn't,' said Mickser morosely. 'They'll have a hard job pinning this on me. I'll fight for my rights. How is Queenie?'

'She's well,' said Finn.

'Listen,' said Mickser. 'I can't help you any more. I'm up here now pretending to be looking at the water below. There's a couple of them half a mile back. I wanted you to see this paper.'

He had a folded newspaper in his hand. He let it fall. Finn picked it up.

'They are on to you, Finn,' he said. 'Get away from here as fast as you can. Keep away from the main roads. Get on to the small by-roads. Follow the sun. Hello, Queenie.'

Derval had come out from inside and was looking up at him.

'Hello, Mister Mickser,' she said.

'I'm sorry I can't accompany you the rest of the way, Queenie,' he said. 'You were a nice travelling companion. Goodbye to you now and good luck. I better go. I've been here long enough. Keep hidden for a while in case they come down to see what I was looking at under the bridge. Good luck to ye. Keep moving, and keep your head down.'

64

Then he pulled away from the bridge and they heard his footsteps over their heads.

Finn sat down on the abutment and opened the folded newspaper. There it was, on the front page, in a sort of black box.

THE FLIGHT OF THE DOVES, it said.

His heart began to beat so fast that he had to close his eyes and not look at it for some time. Derval stood by him and put her hand on his shoulder. Then he read it again. It was quite short. Mr Tobias Morgan was the heartbroken stepfather and legal guardian of the Doves. They had left home. Thinking they might have been removed by Irish relations they had been declared Wards of Court in both countries. Anybody who harboured them, or did not disclose their whereabouts was now in danger of Contempt of Court. Also the heartbroken Mr Morgan was offering a reward of One Hundred Pounds for information that would lead to their being found. He was surprised that the children had been free for so long. He worried about the little girl, and the hardship she must be suffering. He didn't think the Irish police were incompetent, he was just surprised it was taking them so long to find the children, and he had come over himself to help in the search, and to greet them when they were found. He agreed the boy, Finn, was of an adventurous nature. His head was full of Celtic dreams; he got this from both his father and mother. Mr Morgan loved the children dearly. He had devoted his life to them. He was heartbroken at their going, and he was aching to have them back with him again.

The boy was aged about twelve with distinctive red

hair. The girl, Derval, was about seven with long fair hair.

A police spokesman said that the children had been traced and it would not be long now until they were returned to their legal guardian.

Finn let the paper rest on his knees while he thought about it. He was very puzzled. Why did Uncle Toby come after them? Where did Uncle Toby get a hundred pounds to put up? And why? Finn didn't think the two of them were worth a hundred pounds.

Then he thought of something nice. Mickser knew about the hundred pounds. It would have been so easy for him to drop a hint to the police. But he didn't. If he had, they would be on their way back to Uncle Toby now.

'Mister Mickser is gone away,' said Derval.

'Mister Mickser is a good man,' said Finn firmly. I don't care about the old copper, he thought. He also thought that Mister Mickser was a great talker and would talk himself out of trouble like that. He'd talk so much they would be glad to get rid of him.

The other part was worrying. Their description.

He opened the bag and got out the food. There wasn't a lot of food left. He wondered how two people could eat so much food in such a short time. He buttered the bread. They had to drink water from the milk bottle. He looked at Derval. She was a bit grubby. He would have to wash her face and hands at least. Then he thought, with a sigh, he would have to do something else as well.

They ate the bread and butter and the few bits of meat they had left, and the fruit. They were now left with the heel of the loaf and some butter. He thought that Derval should be getting hot food, that all this cold stuff couldn't be good for her. But she looked fairly well.

'I'll have to wash you, Derval,' he said.

'Oh, Finn,' she said.

'It'll have to be done,' he said. 'We are both dirty.'

'Oh, all right,' she said reluctantly.

He took off some of her upper clothes and they went to the river and he washed her hands and her face with a handkerchief. She made faces and kept her eyes shut while he did so. Derval was glad he had no soap.

'Derval,' he said then, 'I will have to do something else with you.'

She looked at him anxiously.

'Something nasty?' she asked.

'I'll have to cut your hair,' he said.

'Why, Finn?' she asked.

'I'll tell you,' he said. 'They are looking for a girl and a boy. The girl has long fair hair and the boy has short red hair. Now if I cut your hair short you will look like a boy. It's only because you have long hair that people can see you are a girl. If we cut your hair short, and you are wearing your long pants, you will be just like a boy, and people will say: Well those are two boys, they are not a girl and a boy. You see?'

She thought over it.

'I'd like to be a boy, so,' she said. 'It will be fun being a boy, Finn, won't it?'

'I hope so,' said Finn. 'All right. Kneel down there in front of me and I'll start cutting it.'

He got Joss's knife. He cleaned it first of the butter and the crumbs. He saw he would have to use the big blade, and on the other side of it when you pulled something a small scissors came out. He was sure it was blunt but he hoped it would do.

'All right now,' he said.

The knife-blade was sharp. He cut at her hair over her ear. It was long silky hair. It wasn't hard to cut, but he didn't like doing it. It was nearly a foot long. He cut it all around her head. Her head looked very odd. Her head looked as if her hair had been hacked off with a knife. It was very ragged. She didn't look like Derval at all. Then he used the scissors to try and make it look respectable. He didn't have a comb so he had to hold the bits with his fingers and cut them with the scissors. It wasn't too blunt. He tried to shape it like a boy's hair, long on top and close cut at the back of the head. He shook his head over it. There were a lot of ridges, but after all it would grow in a few days.

'Now,' he said.

She shook her head.

'It's funny,' she said, 'not to feel my hair.'

'You look just like a boy,' he said. 'Now you will have to have a new name. What name would you like?'

She was pleased with this. She clapped her hands.

'I am Terry Dove,' she said.

'We mustn't forget,' he said. 'Just in case we meet people. We mustn't call you Derval.'

'I'm Terry,' she said.

'We'll go now, so,' he said. When she had the short coat with the hood on it and her trousers, she did look like a boy. It wasn't much of a disguise, he thought, but it was something. And he would have to keep his own hair covered all the time. He had this cap with earflaps. When he put this on and let the earflaps fall, you would never know what colour hair he had. He threw Derval's hair into the flowing river and watched it sail slowly away. Then he packed the clothes into a bundle, the ones they didn't need to use.

They came out from under the arch to the field on the other side. He knew that if he crossed this field and another field and maybe another they would come to some by-road that fed itself into the main road. Before they left he got out his geography book, and he looked at the map of Ireland.

He had seen the name of the town where Mickser was captured. He had a long search for it now on the small map. The map had only the names of the principal towns and the principal roads and railroads but it had the railroad that led to the west. He saw that they would have to travel in a north-west direction in order to reach the railway line. When they reached it, they could follow it by all the back roads. He was glad he had been taught map-reading in school, but he was sorry it was such a small map and carried such little information.

He put it in the bag with a sigh.

Then he took Derval's hand and walked into the field. It was bounded by high dikes with trees growing on top of the dikes. He saw that all the fields were the same. So there was good cover in them as long as they kept away from houses.

There were no cattle in this field.

But he wasn't afraid of cattle, or bulls, even. They would stay near the dike and jump up on it if a bull came thundering at them.

'We are on our own now,' he told Derval, 'and maybe we are better off.'

'We'll go to Granny?' she asked.

'We will,' he said with great determination, as they set off across the field.

But the detective, Michael, had heard a strange story from one of his colleagues about the fall of Mickser, and he was moving fast to have an interview with him.

Chapter Nine

I'm as innocent as a baby,' said Mickser. 'It's just that I have a trusting nature. How was I to know that Baldy had bought copper from somebody who had flogged it? Baldy was innocent too.'

'Excuse me while I laugh,' said Michael.

'You must lead a miserable life,' said Mickser, 'never trusting anybody.'

'I'm not interested in the copper business,' said Michael.

'Oh,' said Mickser, 'and what brought you around?'

'I'm told you had two children in the van with you,' said Michael.

'I did?' Mickser asked.

'So I'm told,' said Michael. 'They were seen, you know.'

'Oh, them,' said Mickser. 'I hate children.'

'Then there were children,' said Michael.

'Yes,' said Mickser, 'a couple of tinker kids wandering the roads. I was giving them a lift to their people's caravan.'

'Even though you hated them?' Michael said.

'You don't have to love them to give them a lift,' said Mickser indignantly.

'Where did you pick them up?' Michael asked.

'I don't know, somewhere on the road,' said Mickser.

71

'It wouldn't have been here in the city?' Michael asked.

'Is it me you're asking?' asked Mickser.

'A policeman on point duty thought he saw two kids in your van at a traffic-light stop,' said Michael.

'They shouldn't recruit men into the police that need glasses,' said Mickser.

'What were they like, those kids?' Michael asked.

'They were like kids,' said Mickser disgustedly.

'What colour hair? Were they boys or girls?'

'Two dirty little chiselers,' said Mickser with a disgusted voice. 'You couldn't tell if they were male or female.'

'Did they have fair hair or red hair or black hair?'

'How could I tell?' said Mickser. 'They might have had blue hair for all I know. I was glad to get rid of them.'

'The men that saw them said one was a little girl with fair hair,' said Michael.

'What's coming over the police at all?' asked Mickser. 'Have they all got weak vision?'

'So they weren't a boy with red hair and a little girl with fair hair?' Michael asked.

'What's wrong with you?' Mickser asked. 'If I had a little girl with fair hair in my van wouldn't I be able to see that and tell you?'

'Would you?' Michael asked.

'Will you go away?' Mickser asked. 'You have taken away my living by impounding my van. Now you want to drive me round the bend with a lot of silly questions. I have to make a living, you know.'

'You could pick up a hundred pounds easily,' said Michael.

72

'Where?' Mickser asked. 'From the Cops Benevolent Fund?'

'If those were the children in your van,' said Michael, 'and you tell me where you saw them last, you will probably get a hundred pounds.'

'If you have nothing else to do, would you drop dead,' said Mickser, 'and let me get on with my business.'

Michael was grinning.

'You know, sometimes you are a good liar, Mickser,' said Michael, 'and other times you are a bad liar.'

'Have you nothing better to do than hounding tinkers' kids?' Mickser asked.

'Wouldn't these kids be better off in a warm home with good food,' asked Michael, 'instead of chasing round like two wild goats?'

'If you say so,' said Mickser.

'Giving nothing away,' said Michael.

'I cannot give what I haven't got,' said Mickser.

Michael left him.

He was almost sure that Mickser had taken the children out of the city in his van. He would have to make certain. He went to the town where Mickser had been nabbed and he asked questions in the police station.

They were almost certain that they had seen two children in the van, but when they caught up with it, there were no children, so there was an element of doubt. It was dark in the alleyways.

What had Mickser done then?

Nothing. When they let him go next morning they had kept an eye on him. He had walked out the main road, leaned on a bridge and then thumbed a lift. He had thumbed about ten cars before a lorry stopped and picked him up.

So Michael inquired about the bridge and walked out there himself.

Why would Mickser be leaning over a bridge, he wondered, as he did the same himself. It wasn't like Mickser to walk half a mile before thumbing a lift. He was very weighty, so why the half-mile? He could have picked up a lift in the town.

Michael climbed over the wall and went down and looked at the river. Then he looked at the arch that was almost free of water and he went in there.

Finn hadn't been tidy enough, he thought, as he found the signs of the food. He walked through the arch and looked at the ground. It was soft ground here, and it was easy to see the two sets of footprints in the mud. They had walked across the mud and on to the grass of the field where their footprints ended.

He went back and sat on the abutment and looked around him. He could tell the whole tale. They had slept, they had eaten and they had washed and they had walked to the other side of the arch so they could hear something that Mickser wanted to say to them. Then while he looked at his feet, he saw something strange. Very delicate strands of hair, he saw as he stooped to pick them up. Long strands of fair hair. So, the little one was now without her hair. What a determined young man he was, this Finn, he thought.

He sat there with his chin in his hands, thinking.

He could go now and follow them and guarantee to have them in a few hours. He wondered why he was so reluctant to do it. Let me reason it out. He had admired the boy, and the way he had performed. It would be such a pity to snatch his break for freedom from him. Michael had met Uncle Toby. Uncle Toby was moving people with his display of tears. After all he had nothing to gain by recovering the two children. Yet he wanted them back desperately. Everyone was affected by him. They were sorry for him.

All the same, Michael had his doubts about him. Nothing concrete. Just the thought that if he was such a good person why had Finn taken off and left him? Something wrong there.

On the other hand it wasn't right for two children, and one of them a little girl, to have to be sleeping out in damp places like this, on the run, no proper food to be got.

He was a detective. He had been told to find the children. This was his duty. Now he knew where they were. They hadn't much of a headstart. It wouldn't require much planning or ingenuity to find them and return them to the aching arms of their Uncle Toby.

He sighed and rose and went out from under the bridge and back to the town.

Then he went back to the city.

It was dark when he got there. His duty-roster was over so he could go home, which he did, and thought some more.

Why wouldn't Mickser pick up a hundred pounds that was there for the taking?

Why had the kids in the street refused to talk about the two children who had played football with them? An absolute dumb silence. Nor had he got even half a clue from the grown-ups in the street.

If Finn was an unpleasant boy, he didn't think this blank wall would have been thrown up. So they must be two attractive children. Then why had they run away from home?

He went into the office in the morning and asked for an interview with his superior. He said a strange thing.

'I have two weeks' holiday coming to me,' he said, 'and I'd like to take them immediately.'

'What's this?' he was asked. 'Did you have a row with the wife?'

'Even if I had one,' said Michael, 'I didn't have a row with her.'

'Nobody goes on holidays this time of the year,' he was told.

'I want to find out what it's like,' said Michael.

'What case are you on?' he was asked.

'Just the two missing kids,' he said.

'Oh, them. Any trace of them?'

'I know the last place they were,' said Michael. 'I have left it in my report. They should be easy to trace.'

'All right,' he was told. 'Be crazy. Crime is quiet at the moment. Send us a postcard.'

'I'll do that,' said Michael. 'Thanks.'

And he left.

Chapter Ten

inn didn't know what the name of this village was.

Finn didn't know what the name of this village was.

He left Derval near a pigsty down the lane off the street of the village. It was a clean pigsty, with small curious pigs in it. The wall was low and Derval could stand on a stone and look in at them. They looked back at her, and came close to the wall with their snouts pointed up at her, giving little grunts. There were about ten of them in it.

'You stay here,' he said. 'I'll just go to a shop and buy a few things. You are not to move.'

'I won't move,' she said, plucking a bit of grass and offering it to one of the pigs. It sniffed it and disdained it. It was well fed.

He left her.

He walked cautiously up the narrow lane. It was quite muddy but his shoes were so muddy now that it made no difference to them. They had no food at all left. For the last day and a half he had been afraid to go anywhere near a village or a small town. They had just walked the fields close to roads, hiding when they heard anybody on the road and proceeding again when they had passed. They gave the lonely houses a wide berth, so wide indeed that they hadn't even once aroused the bark of a dog. But they hadn't travelled far this way. All the roundabout was losing miles on them. He had decided that after today they would get on a big road and walk it, in the hope that they were outside the searchers' net that would have been thrown around the countryside near the bridge. But to do that they would have to eat first.

He walked cautiously up the lane, and came on to the road and looked. It was a small village. There were only about twelve houses. One of them, halfway up the street, was a modern shop with a big window that looked strange set into an old-fashioned house.

As he walked towards it he was fingering the money in his pocket and wondering what was the best thing to buy. Bread and butter, and some fruit, which was very dear. Maybe he should buy some eggs for Derval but they would be hard to carry without breaking, and some meat anyhow, out of a tin or cooked, so that she would have something substantial to eat. Chocolate for sure.

He looked at the window of the shop. There were so many nice things in the window that they were beginning to confuse him. But the prices were marked and he started to add up in his head how much he could afford out of his few shillings.

Determined, he walked towards the entrance. He hadn't noticed a car coming down the street, but he noticed it now, for staring at him with his mouth open was Uncle Toby.

As Uncle Toby shouted, 'Stop,' to the driver who was a policeman, Finn turned and ran.

He heard the car stopping and starting again and he heard the voice of Uncle Toby calling.

He thought he would never reach the mouth of the lane. His heart was pounding madly. His breath was short, but then he was there and he turned running.

Behind he heard the screech of brakes as the car stopped. It could never come down this narrow lane. He heard the voice of Uncle Toby calling, 'Finn! Finn!'

He ran around the bend. Derval was still looking in at the pigs. He grabbed her hand. 'Run! Run!' he said and pulled her after him. She couldn't run fast. How could she? She had such small legs. He knew Uncle Toby couldn't run fast either, but the policeman who was with him in the car looked young. Finn prayed that he was fat, but he didn't think so.

He had to slow down for Derval. She was running as fast as she could. The lane twisted a lot, and then they came to the place where it was bisected by a slow-moving river. The river looked clean and ran over gravel. He bent down. 'On my back!' he said to her. She put her arms around his neck, and he ran straight into the river. This was brave of him because he didn't know how deep it was. It slowed him down and he felt it wet in his shoes and his socks and up to his legs, up, up until it was past his knees.

It didn't go any higher, and he was soon free and into the lane again, and as he saw a turn-off to the left he took it and ran, Derval still on his back. But there was despair in his heart, because he knew he couldn't outrun them. They were only a few minutes behind, and he was panting hard, his head down.

So he didn't see the man he ran into, but he heard the 'Oops!' a sort of grunt as they nearly knocked him down.

Finn stopped. What was the use? It was all over. He looked at the man. He wore a hat and a thick jersey and a coat and trousers tucked into his socks and he carried a pack on his back and a home-made walking-stick in his hand.

'Someone after you?' he asked.

Finn couldn't answer. He just nodded his head.

They were beside a dike that sheltered a field. There was a gate into the field, but the man didn't hesitate. He took Derval from Finn. 'Over the dike,' he said, and went over himself, carrying Derval.

Inside the gate there was a big stack of turf that the farmer had built, for his winter supply, nicely dried by the sun, sods built up into the shape of a pan loaf. But it was deceptive, as Finn saw. The man ran to the end of it, and here there was an opening where a horse-cart rested on its shafts. Finn followed the man in here and he had to sit on the ground to recover his breath. The man let Derval down on her feet and they listened. They heard the sound of running feet and the calling voice of Uncle Toby: 'Finn! Here I am. Come to me, dear boy! Finn! Finn! It's your own Uncle Toby.'

Finn was looking at the face of the man. The hat was back off his forehead. He had a square sort of face. He was grinning. He winked at Finn. Finn didn't know why, but this wink suddenly and immediately restored all his courage.

We are not caught yet, he thought. There is still hope for us. They listened in silence as the calling voice faded away.

Finn looked at the man.

'My name is Michael,' the man said. 'I am hiking about the place. On a holiday.'

'I am Finn,' Finn said, 'and this is my sis— my brother Terry.'

'Pleased to meet you,' Michael said. 'Hello, Terry.'

80

Derval looked at him solemnly for a while and then she smiled.

'You don't want to meet the man who is calling your name?' Michael asked.

'No,' said Finn.

'We better move, so,' Michael said. 'Out there is a very big bog. If we can cross this bog and get to the network of roads on the other side we will have a good two day start on them. They will stay searching this side because they won't think you could cross the bog. Will we go?'

'All right,' said Finn.

'We will keep behind the voice for a little while,' said Michael. 'Let us hope that he keeps calling.'

They came out of the carthouse cautiously, and went to the gate and listened. They could still hear the voice of Uncle Toby calling.

'Good,' Michael said and they went into the lane. They walked up the lane, still listening. Michael seemed to be able to trace the movements of the others by the sound of the voice. He stopped at the place where the river bisected the lane. This made him look at Finn's feet.

'You are very wet,' he said.

'But we are still free,' said Finn.

Michael listened once more. The sound of the voice had stopped now. 'They will go to the car now,' he said, 'and circle around the area. So we will head for the bog.'

He turned left and they followed him.

About half a mile of twisting and winding lanes were behind them when they came on to the great bog. It seemed to stretch to the horizon. Away off to the left of them they saw a big station with water-cooling towers sending great clouds of steam into the sky. Here for miles the bog was brown where it had been cut over with giant machines.

'They make electricity down there,' Michael said. 'We'll go this other way.' This was a great part of bog that was covered in heather and tufts of green sedge and on the hard ground there were furze bushes growing with yellow-coloured blossoms on them. 'Could you carry my pack?' Michael asked.

'I could,' said Finn.

'The going will be soft,' said Michael. 'I will have to carry the little brother.'

He stripped himself of the pack and put it on Finn's back. It was quite heavy. Michael tightened the straps on his shoulders, and then bent and said to Derval, 'Up now.' Derval hesitated a little but then put her arms around his neck, and he tucked her legs around his waist with his arms. 'Follow me closely,' he said to Finn.

They set off into the bog.

Finn noticed that he chose low ground between little hillocks, so that if anybody was looking out over the bog from a height they would be hidden by the folds. This low ground was very wet and soggy. Now and again they came on sort of roads that had been built into the bog from the sides. Here there were turf banks, with bogholes in front of them, where men still cut out turf with the slean, and you could see the marks of the slean in the high banks.

Finn didn't know how many miles they had travelled, but the pack on his back seemed to get heavier and heavier. The sun was behind a mist and it was very hot. There was no wind. The bog-larks were high in the sky, singing. It was almost impossible to see them. Now and again fluttering snipe got up almost from under their feet

His eyes were almost closed with the tiredness when he heard Michael say, 'We will stop here.'

He looked around him. It was a place where turf-cutters had been working. There were freshly cut sods of turf laid out in long rows to dry. The turf-cutters had made themselves comfortable when they were there. They had cut a sort of cave out of last year's high bank. There were three railway sleepers around the three sides of it, and it was floored with dry heather and last year's sedge. In front of it there was a hearth they had made with stones, and the white ashes of former turf fires were still there.

'You are tired, Terry,' Michael said to her.

'Oh, no,' she said.

'Here,' he said. 'You go into this nice cave and lie on the bench.' He brought her in. He had felt her head nodding on his back as he carried her. 'You lie down there for a little while,' he said. 'And we'll cook up something good for you.' He stripped off his own coat and put it on the bench. She climbed up without his assistance and lay down. Almost while he was looking at her she was asleep.

'Change your pants,' he said to Finn. 'Have you a change with you?'

'I have another trousers and socks,' said Finn.

'Change,' said Michael. 'I'll light a fire and you can dry them.'

Finn went into the cave and opened his bundle.

Michael got last year's turf from around the bank and in no time at all he had a turf fire going. Finn watched in amazement as he took a kettle and a pan from the pack. He went and collected water from a little trickle that was flowing from the ground into a boghole. When the fire was going well, he broadened it so that it would hold both the kettle and the pan, and then he proceeded to take huge chunks of steak from the pack and he put those on the pan. Also he had three plastic plates and three plastic cups. Idly it entered into Finn's head why he should have three of those things, but the smell of the cooking was so pleasant that the saliva started to run from his teeth. Michael had bread and butter, and when the steaks were nearly done, he plopped thick slices of bread into the hot fat.

He was laughing at the look on Finn's face.

'Why are you laughing?' Finn asked.

'You look so hungry,' he said.

'Why do you have such good things when you are hiking?' Finn asked.

'It's only young hikers,' said Michael, 'that don't think of their stomachs. When I hike, I like to hike in comfort. Will your brother come out now? At this stage, I think he needs food more than sleep.'

Later they sat in front of the fire. Their seats were sods of dried turf packed together. They made nice enough seats. Finn thought he had never tasted better food in his life. It was coming on to twilight time. The fire was making their faces glow.

Michael was smoking a cigarette. Then he put his hand in his pack and took out a paper.

'Read that, Finn,' he said.

Finn looked at him, startled, and then he looked at the newspaper.

GRANNY O'FLAHERTY DEFIANT

it said.

It went on to say that the flying Doves were still at liberty despite an intense police search and the offering of a reward. Mrs Grainne O'Flaherty, the grandmother of the children, had been asked if she would shelter the children if they succeeded in reaching her. She said she didn't give a traneen for their supposed guardian or the supposed guardianship of the courts. If her grandchildren reached her, nobody would take them away except over her dead body. Asked if they were with her now, she replied that even an O'Flaherty Dove couldn't fly that fast. She was expecting them every day at Carraigmore.

That's it,' said Finn involuntarily, 'that's the name, Carraigmore.' Then he put his hand over his mouth as he looked at Michael. Then he took it down. 'Do you know?' he asked.

'It would be hard for me not to,' Michael said. 'You bump into me. I read the papers. You have red hair.'

'But why are you helping us, so?' asked Finn.

'How do I know?' Michael asked. 'I don't like people chasing kids or something. What does it matter? We'll sleep here tonight. We'll finish crossing the bog tomorrow, and then we will part and you'll go your way and I'll go mine. Isn't that fair enough?'

'You will go away?' Derval asked suddenly.

'I have to,' he said. 'You will be going west, and I will be going east. I have people to see. But who knows, maybe our paths will cross again.'

'I'm sorry you are not coming with us to Granny,' said Derval.

85

'You have nothing to worry about,' said Michael. 'Finn will look after you. He is doing very well.'

'If it wasn't for you we would have been caught,' said Finn.

'How do you know?' Michael asked. 'Something else might have happened. You might have got away. If a fellow wants a thing badly enough, he will get it. Will you tell me why you want so badly to get to Carraigmore?'

Finn looked at him. Michael's eyes were calm and kind, he thought. He wouldn't be a one to go and tell the police he saw you for the sake of a hundred pounds. He picked up a piece of turf and rolled it between his hands.

Then he tried to explain to Michael why he wanted to get to Carraigmore.

Well, he has convinced me, anyhow, Michael thought, and it was as well that I caught up with him. Looking at the thin earnest face, with the freckled nose and the firm chin, and hearing the unexaggerated account of life with Uncle Toby, he was glad he had made his decision. But this was not the end of the road. There was a long way between here and Carraigmore and the law and courts were powerful things, very difficult to circumvent.

He could put them in a car now and deliver them to Granny O'Flaherty. But that would be breaking the law, and after all he was the law. He was bending the law now but not breaking it or he would have to resign from the police. He intended to cross the sea, meet the Inspector, and investigate Uncle Toby, talk to his neighbours, and find out what was compelling him in the pursuit of the children. He couldn't believe it was love, somehow. Because the arm of the law was long, and it would reach out for the children no matter where they ended up. Even if he brought them straight to their destination now, the law would be there.

He would have to be prepared to meet the law with the truth. This was what the law was about. Truth had no law to fight. He hoped the children could keep free for the time he required to find the truth that would really free them. He thought, with Finn's determination, that they might.

'I will have to leave you in the morning,' he said. He saw that Finn was upset. 'I must,' he said. 'It will be only for a few days. I want to find out important things that will be good for you in the long run. But I will catch up with you again.'

'You will?' said Finn.

'I promise,' he said. 'You'll see me again when you least expect me.'

Then he gave Finn a better map, marked.

'Don't follow the railroad,' he said. 'They will be watching that. Go north from the railroad, and get across the Shannon away from the railroad. You see the river. There are different bridges. They will be watching the bridges.' He waited until he was sure Finn knew the best route. 'When you cross the river and get into the mountains, Granny O'Flaherty will be reaching out for you.'

Next morning when they crossed the bog and got on to the roads on the other side, he left them. They were sorry to see him go, but out of his pack he had loaded their own bags with food and tins, enough to keep them going for a few days.

They waved goodbye after him.

I don't care, Finn was thinking, I am going to get to Carraigmore.

They set out to walk west. Michael sat down to wait until they were out of sight.

Chapter Eleven

Normally, children run away from home quite often. Either they change their minds after a short time and go home again, or after a short search they are found and returned. Sometimes those escapades are reported in the local paper if they last long enough to be news. Most times they don't.

Unknown to Finn, the flight of the Doves was causing a lot of reporting, mainly because it was lasting so long. It had all the ingredients of a serial. The children should have been found easily and the story should have died, but they weren't caught and it lived.

As far as Finn was concerned this was good and bad. Most people were on the side of the children, hoping they would succeed in finishing their journey. Many of the nation were gamblers, and they bet on this at even money: that the children would reach the west, or they would be found before they got there. Granny O'Flaherty was a colourful person, and the newspapers were delighted with her. Finn didn't know this: passing through places that seemed to be bare of people, he had many times been seen by the unseen eyes of the country. The element of doubt was introduced because the little girl didn't look like a girl, but was definitely a boy. This had helped.

But all the publicity was bad in this way, that the police felt their searching was becoming a joke, and they were becoming annoyed. Instead of saying to a policeman friend: Why are you never around when you are wanted, the joke now was: You couldn't catch a dove.

So at the top level there was annoyance and this was passed down through the lower levels: Bring in those children. So there was rather intense activity, and as Finn and Derval came nearer and nearer to the west, so the search for them could be concentrated in a smaller area, and as they came closer to the great Shannon river that was like a huge dike of river and lakes separating the west from the rest of the country, the attention of the authorities was directed at the bridges that crossed the river, and since there were only about a dozen in a great area stretching from Limerick in the south to Lough Allen in the north, it didn't require many men to watch those crossings, while the rest closed in from the rear. In fact there was no way anybody saw how the children could cross the river (except by boat in the dark of the night) and not be spotted.

Well, they got across the bridge, but in an extraordinary way.

They were walking in this laneway. It was rough. Finn noticed that Derval was very tired. She had been very good. One night they had slept in a hayshed. Another night they had slept in an empty cowbyre. This was a place where there were wooden stalls where they put the hay for the cattle. They had slept in the stalls, on the hay that was left. It had been raining hard that night, so the stalls were comfortable and they could hear the rain beating heavily on the tin roof.

They were walking now in this deeply rutted lane, when they came to the donkey.

He was a big donkey. He was cropping the long grass on the side of the laneway. He was blocking the lane in fact. He was nearly as big as a jennet. He wouldn't get out of the way, so Finn had to lean against him, pushing at his hindquarters, so that they would have room to pass. They passed him.

They had walked some way when Derval was suddenly pushed forward and nearly fell. Finn was astonished to see that the donkey had come up behind her and butted her in the back with his head. As soon as she straightened herself, he gave her another butt.

'Here,' said Finn, 'stop that! What are you doing?' just as if the donkey could understand what he was saying. The way he pushed the little girl wasn't vicious, but playful. It seemed an extraordinary thing for the donkey to do. He followed her again now and she had to go behind Finn.

The donkey wasn't in the least afraid of them, Finn noticed. He just stood there watching them, waiting for Derval to come out of hiding so that he could butt her again. When Finn put his hand on his head, he didn't move. When Finn started to scratch him behind one of his long ears, he enjoyed it. He was the first really friendly donkey that Finn had met, except suddenly he now remembered the donkey with Granny O'Flaherty. He had gone with this donkey to collect dry turf from the bog. The donkey had two baskets each side of a pannier. He had been a small donkey and just trudged away and was very pleased if he got a few grains of sugar that were left over from the lunch.

Suddenly Finn thought that this donkey might be of help to them. He searched his bag and took a handful of sugar from the little that remained. He held it in his palm and the donkey sniffed it and then ate it with great relish and nudged Finn on the shoulder.

'Up with you,' said Finn, taking Derval and putting her on the donkey's back. Then he got up behind her himself. The donkey turned his head to look back at them. 'On with you,' said Finn. 'Go, donkey,' and he tapped the donkey's body with his heels. He was afraid for a moment that the donkey would suddenly start bucking, but he didn't. He seemed to shrug his shoulders and then ambled off in the lane, seemingly quite content.

Finn was delighted. It was nice to be carried. He realized that he was tired himself. He wondered who the donkey belonged to. They would hardly miss him if they had allowed him to wander away like this, and the donkey could walk faster than they could.

'You like this?' he asked Derval.

'Ye-e-es,' said Derval doubtfully. She was a bit afraid of the donkey.

'He was only playing when he pushed you,' said Finn.

'He's very spiney,' said Derval.

'We'll fix that,' said Finn. 'Whoa, donkey,' he shouted. The donkey didn't whoa, so Finn got off his back and held him by the head. Then he made a sort of soft seat for Derval out of their spare clothes, and she was more satisfied when she sat back. So Finn mounted the donkey again, said, 'Go, donkey,' and the donkey obeyed him and ambled off.

They came to a main road that was tarred. Finn decided to take a chance and he turned the donkey's head with light blows of his hand on his neck, and the donkey walked on the grass verge. There wasn't much traffic, an occasional car or a lorry. It was a very pleasant day. There was just a light breeze and the sun was warm when it came out from behind the white fleecy clouds.

He looked at his map. He wondered where Michael was now, and what lucky chance had made them meet with him in the first place. He saw from the map that they were only about five miles from the smallish town that was built near the bridge over the big river. He decided that they would get as close as possible to the town, and see how they would cross afterwards.

They rode the donkey this way for about an hour. After that Finn found that the donkey's back was hurting him, so he got down and walked beside the donkey holding Derval with his arm.

When he saw a church spire in the distance, he turned the donkey off the main road, and went into a small road on the right that curved around towards the left. He thought that it would eventually lead to the town if they followed it.

The sun was low in the sky now. When he could see some of the houses coloured by the sun, and the windows reflecting its light blindingly, he came on a gate that opened easily. It led into a field, and about fifty yards from the gate a river flowed, but it wasn't the big river but a tributary, and near the bank of this river there was an old broken-down stone house. Nothing remained of it except the walls and the opening into it and one chimney. It had long ago been cleared of the rubble and acted as a shelter for sheep. Soft grass grew where the floor of the house had been. Near the house there was a big old tree, and surrounding this tree on the ground were many of its branches that had been blown down when they rotted, and he saw that there was plenty of wood to make a fire.

'Will you stay here?' he asked Derval. 'Inside the old house. I must go into the town and look, and buy some things.'

'I would be afraid of the donkey,' she said.

'He won't do anything to you,' said Finn. 'Look, he's too busy eating the grass now to bother with you. I won't be long. Sit with your back near the fireplace, and then he won't do anything to you. I'll be back before you finish counting up to a hundred.'

'All right, Finn,' she said.

She sat beside the place where the big open fire used to be. The chimney still remained, but a lot of it had fallen down. Watching her sitting there patiently, Finn wondered again if he had been right to bring her on this adventure. Thinking of her at home with Uncle Toby, if he had run on his own, made up his mind for him and he waved at her, ran to the gate, closed it and ran towards the town, halting when he got near it to pull the cap down far on his head to hide his hair. Then he slowed his pace and walked through the town until he came to the bridge over the river.

He stood at a corner and looked over at it.

There was a policeman leaning with his elbows on the wall, talking to a man in a fawn coat. They were laughing, but all the same he noticed that the policeman was looking at everyone that passed, and very significantly, he would bend down to look at any car coming from the east that had children in it.

If this wasn't enough, he saw another policeman come along and talk to the two men, and then the first policeman went away with the man with the fawn coat, and the second one leaned his elbows on the walls of the bridge and looked carefully at everyone passing by.

Now he knew.

He walked towards the bridge, but he didn't cross. He went to the right of it and looked at the river. It was very broad and very deep. If they couldn't walk across by the bridge, he thought that tomorrow they would walk along the banks of the river, for however long it took, in the hope that somewhere along its length they might come on a boat that they could borrow. As far as he could see, it was the only way to cross the river.

He went into a shop where you got a basket and took things from the shelf and paid for them on the way out. This suited him. There was nobody to look closely at you, like the people behind the counters in ordinary shops. He bought biscuits and chocolate and milk and a tin of meat. He paid a girl at a little desk. She just looked at what was in the basket and put the price on to a machine, and he paid and she didn't even look at him.

He was dismayed to see how little money he had left. We will have to get to Granny O'Flaherty's soon, he thought, or we will be in trouble. Unless he tried to take things that he couldn't pay for. If he had to, he thought, he would do that, and pay for them again when they had reached safety.

He hurried back to the place he had left Derval. It was getting dark now. The lights were on in the streets of the town.

'I counted to five hundred,' said Derval.

'I'm sorry,' he said, 'I got here as fast as I could. I'll

get sticks now and we will light a fire in the old chimneyplace and eat a marvellous supper.'

He collected the sticks. They were very dry and brittle. He got wrapping paper from his bag, and set fire to that, and the wood blazed in the old chimney.

It was very cheerful. It lighted the place up, and when the warmth started to come from it, even the donkey came over to graze near it.

They got the benefit of the fire, but they didn't succeed in getting to eat their supper.

Chapter Twelve

One moment they were there alone with the donkey in the firelight and the next moment they seemed to be surrounded by young people, as if they had grown from the grass.

Finn was startled.

'You stole Moe!' this chap said to him. He was as tall as Finn. He had black curly hair falling over his forehead. He was not very clean. He was wearing other people's clothes that had been cut down or something. He had a stick in his hand and he was pointing this at Finn. There were at least six other children with him, a girl in a very ragged dress, and three boys and a small girl. They were all panting after running, he could see. This boy was very belligerent. He was in his bare feet and his legs were spread and he was crouching.

'Who's Moe?' Finn asked.

'Who's Moe? Who's Moe?' he asked in great scorn. 'As if you didn't know who Moe was. I'll learn you who Moe is.'

He came forward determinedly with the stick raised. Derval got behind Finn as he rose. Finn bent down and took one of the big sticks from the fire. It was burning, but then it stopped and started to smoke. It was a good stout stick.

'Imagine goin' to hit a fella with a burning stick,' the boy said indignantly.

97

'You were going to hit me,' said Finn.

'I was and I wasn't,' the boy said. 'If somebody stole Moe on you, what would you do?'

'I don't know who Moe is,' said Finn.

'You don't know Moe,' said the boy pointing at the donkey, 'and you after stealing him?'

'Oh,' said Finn. 'You mean the donkey. I didn't know he was Moe.'

'Well you know now,' said the boy. 'Why did you steal him?'

'We were walking,' said Finn. 'We have walked a long way. We were tired and we saw Moe. This was miles away. So I put my little brother on his back, and he carried us this way.'

'And what were you goin' to do with him? Sell him in the next town, eh?' the boy asked.

'Indeed I would do no such thing,' said Finn. 'We would have left him here in the field.'

'And the farmer would get the police after him,' said the boy. 'And they'd put him in the pound and me father'd have to pay to get him out.'

'How would I know all those things?' Finn asked. 'I only borrowed him for a little while.'

Suddenly the other children started laughing. The boy looked around. There was Moe and he was bending down and butting the little girl with his head, chasing her all around the small space.

She was saying, 'Stop, Moe! Stop, Moe.'

The boy laughed. He went over to Moe and caught him by the head.

'Isn't he gas?' he asked. 'See what he does to Sheila. He'll always do that with little girls. I don't know why.'

'I know,' said Finn. 'He did it to my little— little brother.'

'That's funny,' the boy said. 'He only used to do it to little girls. What's your brother's name?'

'Terry,' said Finn.

'I'm Moses,' the boy said. 'My father called the donkey after me. Big Moses and little Moe. You see?'

'That's funny,' said Finn. 'I'm Joseph,' saying his second name.

'Well, as long as you didn't mean any harm,' Moses said. 'We won't fight with ye.' He put little Sheila on the donkey's back. Two of the small fellas got up behind her.

'We didn't hurt Moe,' said Finn.

'Where are ye goin'? What are ye doin'?' Moses asked.

'We are just travelling,' said Finn.

'Where's yer people?' Moses asked.

'We have no people,' said Finn.

'How can ye have no people?' Moses asked. 'Everybody has people.'

'Our people are dead,' said Finn. 'We have a granny over in the west. We are travelling to her.'

'Oh,' said Moses. He screwed up his eyes, looking at Finn. 'We are going across tonight. Would you like to come with us?'

'You are going across the river?' Finn asked.

'Yeh,' he said. 'We been here too long now. We'll move on and on. We always cross the Shannon this time and go round and round for the races in Connacht.'

Finn thought it was a miracle. There were so many of them. Who would see two more going across the bridge in the midst of them?

'Would your people mind us going with you?' he asked.

'Nah,' said Moses. 'What does it matter?'

'We were going to cook our food,' said Finn.

'Bring it with you,' Moses said. 'We ha' a big pot. Here, put your brother up on Moe.'

He went to reach for Derval. She shrank away from him.

It didn't deter him, Finn saw with surprise. He crouched down in front of her.

'I won't hurt you,' he said. 'I just want you to go on Moe's back with my brothers. Will you do that, heh? We will get to the camp quicker if you and the small ones are not walking.'

Derval looked at Finn. He wanted her to make her own decision. It seemed to him that Moses was all right.

Derval went with Moses. He took her hand and hoisted her up on Moe's back. Finn gathered their bags and stuff.

The big girl led Moe out of the house and towards the gate. Moses stayed with Finn until he was ready.

'You are from away,' he said. 'You don't speak like real people.'

'Over the sea,' said Finn, as they walked out after the others.

'I thought you didn't speak like real people,' said Moses.

They closed the gate after them, and followed the others right down into the town, towards the bridge, and then they turned left down by the river. Finn noticed that not a head was turned to look at them. It was an odd sight, four children riding a donkey and yet nobody noticed. Because they were tinker's children, he supposed, like why should you look at a postman? He hoped that Moses' father would be friendly to them.

They were camped a few hundred yards down by the river, on a waste piece of land beside the last light out of the town. Finn saw that they had a caravan, with a round top and parts of it painted in yellow and red. There were several pinto ponies, hobbled, and a flat sort of cart, and two tents, round ones made of bent sticks with black tarpaulin thrown over them. The place wasn't clean. There were many old rags and things around and rusted tins, and they had a couple of greyhounds.

Moses' father was sitting near the fire of sticks. His mother was bending over a pot there.

The father looked like Moses. He had curly hair, and his shirt was open and he had thick hair on his chest. He had a few-days-old beard on him and his teeth looked very white on that account. He had a big bone in his hand and was eating the meat off it.

'Powder, this is Joseph and his brother,' said Moses. 'He wants to come with us a little way.'

Powder looked him over, from his head to his toes. He had shrewd eyes.

'You've travelled,' he said.

'We are travelling to the west,' said Finn.

The lady at the pot sat back on her heels. She had black hair too, that was tight and shiny on her head, with a split in the centre of it. She looked a young woman. She smiled at Finn.

'You will get something to eat soon,' she said.

'You found Moe,' Powder said.

'Yeh, he was wandering,' said Moses.

There was a commotion then. The children had got down from the donkey's back, and as soon as Derval

101

had landed and was walking towards Finn, Moe came behind her and started to butt her. They laughed.

'I never saw him do that to a boy,' said Moses.

'Ho-ho,' said Powder, as Finn went to rescue Derval. When Finn brought her back, Powder said, 'Moe thinks you are a little girl, young one.'

'He is so fair,' Moses' mother said, rubbing a finger on Derval's cheek. 'Many girls would die to have fair skin like that. We will eat now,' she called to the others.

They gathered around the fire. The mother handed out tin mugs to them when she had dipped them in the pot and filled them. The children started to dip into their mugs with their fingers, popping meat into their mouths and then shaking their fingers.

Finn tried it. It was very hot. He found if you dipped fast and put it into your mouth fast your fingers weren't scalded. He tried it once or twice. Then he saw that they were looking at him and their eyes were laughing.

'We will give the little fellow a plate,' Moses' mother said. 'He hasn't been trained to our ways.' She filled a tin plate for Derval and gave her a spoon.

What harm but it was good, Finn thought, as he savoured it. He got the hang of it. He would eat a piece of meat with his fingers and then sip some of the scalding soup and potatoes.

When they had finished one mug, she filled it again for them.

Finn thought it was nice to be sitting in the light of the big fire, and eating out of tin mugs. Then the mother gave them hunks of bread. It was a filling meal.

Powder said, 'Now you will break up', and the children went and started to do a lot of things, breaking the tents and folding them, gathering things that were on the bushes, catching one of the ponies and tackling him and putting him under the shafts of the caravan.

'Can I help them?' Finn asked.

'No,' said Powder. 'You'd be in the way of them. You have come far?'

For some reason Finn was cautious.

'A fair way,' he said.

'It's strange to see two kids like you on the road,' Powder said.

'We had no money,' said Finn. 'It was easier to walk. People gave us lifts. They were kind to us, like you.'

Powder grunted. He was picking his teeth with a match.

'You are welcome,' he said. 'You have never travelled with people like us before?'

'No,' said Finn.

Powder laughed.

'You will learn a lot,' he said. 'Can you read and write?'

'Yes,' said Finn.

'Can you write better than you talk?' Powder asked.

'I don't know,' said Finn.

Powder laughed again, rose to his feet.

'All right,' he called. 'Let us get on the road.'

Finn noticed that Powder himself did not work. He stood and shouted, 'Do this! Do that!' The children and the woman were very expert. They had done it many times before. Moe was tackled and put into the shafts of the small flat cart. Most of the tents and some of the utensils were packed on to this. A lot of stuff went into the caravan. The greyhounds were tied on long leads from the axle of the caravan, and then the lot was set under way. Powder walked at the head of the pony with the caravan. Then came the cart. Moses walked at Moe's head and Finn walked beside him. The small children with Derval were up on the cart.

His heart beat faster all the same when they turned on to the bridge. There was a policeman there. Finn kept his eyes averted from him until they were passing him, and then when he looked he saw with relief that there was nothing but disinterest in his eyes as he watched the passage of the tinker column.

They were across the bridge, and whatever happened now, they were that much nearer Granny O'Flaherty.

Chapter Thirteen

When he woke up the next morning it took Finn some time to work out where he was. He could hear birds singing and the sound of a river running over stones.

He was lying beside Derval on a sackful of straw. Over his head he saw the bottom boards of the cart, and when he stretched out his hand he could touch the slender wheel.

They had travelled for about three hours the evening before. Then they had set up their camp near a river in a grove of tall trees which was a part of the land that was left by the roadside when they had taken a bend out of the road to widen it. The first thing that had gone up was the tent for Powder. As soon as that was ready, he had gone in to sleep, while the woman and the children set up the rest of the camp. Powder didn't seem to be very active, Finn saw, but none of them complained about this. He was a pampered Powder, and his children were very fond of him.

Finn looked at his hands, which were dirty, and then at Derval's face, which was grubby. He shook her.

'Come on,' he said, 'we must go and wash.'

'Oh, Finn,' she said protestingly.

'Not, Finn,' he said. 'You must call me Joseph, remember.'

'All right,' she said, rubbing her eyes. Her hands were dirty too.

They came out from under the cart. It was a nice morning. The sun was warm. Moses was bent at the fire blowing on the sticks. He was the only one up and about.

'Hello,' said Finn. 'You are lighting the fire.'

'Yeh,' said Moses. 'Where ye goin'?'

'We are going to wash in the river,' said Finn.

'What would ye be doin' a thing like that for?' Moses asked.

'We just want to be clean,' said Finn.

Moses shook his head.

'There's no money in that,' he said sagely.

Finn laughed and went on to the river. It was a nice place. It was very shallow and ran over stones. It was clear. The tall trees rose up from the ground all around.

Derval made terrible faces while he washed her. His own hands were so dirty that he had to use a little gravel to get the dirt out of the creases. Moses had come over and was squatting on the ground watching him.

'You won't get nothin' by bein' clean, Joseph,' he said.

'What do you mean?' Finn asked him.

'Ach, you'll see,' he said. 'They expect you to be dirty. The dirtier you are the better.'

When they got back, the woman, Moses' mother, was up and getting the breakfast.

'You are hungry?' she said to Finn, smiling.

'Yes,' he said.

'It's like the young birds,' she said. 'Children are always hungry.'

106

She made tea and gave them chunks of bread. The bread was mostly heels of loaves, some of it brown and some of it white. She took them out of a sack she had. They were what she got when she sent the children begging at farmers' houses. He had seen them doing that last night.

He got to know what Moses meant about being clean, when he went with him into the small town after their breakfast. Derval stayed behind playing with the small girl, Sheila. She seemed quite content to do so. Moses and his sister, Eileen, and the other kids went to the town.

It was a small town and it was market day. In the square there were many carts from which the farmers were selling eggs and chickens and vegetables. The children spread out all over the place and stood with their hands out. Moses was very good at it, Finn saw. He started outside the church where people were coming from the late Mass. He just stood there in his ragged clothes, holding out a dirty hand. Some people were annoyed with him. A boy like you begging in the streets! Why don't you work for a living? What kind of a lazy father have you at all? Moses, with a blank face just kept saying, 'Help us, please. We are hungry.' He didn't answer any of the sociological questions that were put to him. He just repeated his plea for help and kept it up. It was amazing how many people in the end, owing to his persistence, put money in his hand.

After the church he joined the others at the market place. 'Now you see why you must be dirty,' he said to Finn. 'If you were clean they wouldn't give you a make.' There was sense in what he said, Finn saw. Sometimes they would have to flee when they saw the uniform of a policeman coming. It was against the law to beg. He saw that some of the other tinker people went around with a cardboard box containing small cheap prints of holy things. Moses informed him that as long as they were holding these things they couldn't be accused of begging, but Moses and his company scorned this way of doing business.

Every hour or so Moses would make a collection from the others, several shillings at a time, and go to the end of the street, where Powder was leaning against a wall, with other men, and he would hand over the money and Powder would count it and go into the pub. So what the children were doing, Finn saw, was keeping Powder in drink-money. He noticed that Moses retained some of the money and before they went back to the camp, when the numbers of people started to thin out, he bought some groceries, bread and meat mainly.

Back at the camp they ate stew again, and as soon as they had finished their meal they started to pack up. It was a good thing that the weather was fine. This time Finn could help in the packing, and as they set out on the road the sun was going down and the sky was a beautiful colour. He thought it was a nice way to travel west, always going towards the sunset, walking beside Moses, watching the caravan in front, listening to the clop of the horses' hooves on the road. He liked the smell of the wood fires, and the sight of the bright flames in the dark of the night. He thought how lucky they were to have found Moses and his family. Being with them was a perfect disguise, because nobody spared them a second glance.

He thought this might last the whole way to the west and the safety of Granny O'Flaherty's house, and he felt gleeful about it, thinking of Uncle Toby and the police scouring the country for them, and they ambling by under their noses, because Moses told him that bit by bit, they would be going to Carraigmore, where they would buy donkeys, which they would take to the North, and get a good price for them there, where they were shipped to North Africa where the Arabs couldn't get enough of them. So it looked all set and fair, and he felt he could relax from the tension, and stop looking over his shoulder.

Alas.

In the evening they came to this spot where there were already three or four or more families of caravans set up. One of the families even had a motor van. It was a big encampment, set in the wind of a river. Some of the families had been there for quite a while, you could see that. They hadn't kept the place very clean. There were many pinto ponies and horses and donkeys wandering each side of the encampment, some of them hobbled. Also some families had billy-goats with long beards.

They set up their own camp, and Powder went over to a big fire where the men were gathered, while the rest of them built up the tents, got a fire going, and Moses' mother made strong tea in the black kettle.

It was an odd sight in the light of the big fires.

The fires died down and people went into their tents, and Finn settled down with Derval on the straw under the cart. He must have fallen asleep.

He awoke to a great confusion of shouting, and when he opened his eyes he saw that it was nearly as bright as day, but a red day, and when he looked through the spokes of the wheel he saw that there were a lot of men surrounding the camp and that they all held blazing torches in their hands. The torches smelled of paraffin oil. They had formed a circle around the whole camp. The tinker men were coming out of their tents and their caravans, rubbing the sleep out of their eyes, only half dressed.

Men were shouting.

One big man with a torch finally made sense to Finn.

'Out now!' he was shouting. 'Away from here now. We are sick of you. A bunch of thieves. Dirty locusts. We are sick of your robbing. Away now. Up and away or we'll drive you out!'

Finn saw Powder appear in the middle. He was swinging his arms. He was shouting. 'Who you think you are? Who you think you are?' He was standing with his legs spread, waving his big arms.

'Out or we'll burn you out!' the big farmer shouted.

Finn saw Powder making for this big man. 'I'll powder you! I'll powder you!' he was shouting. As he got near the big farmer another man came out of the torch line, a stick rose and fell and Powder collapsed on the road.

'We don't want trouble,' the farmer shouted. 'Pack up and go, that's all we ask. Pack up and go now, or take what's coming to you!'

Finn could see the tinker men undecided. There was a very tense pause, and then Moses' mother went to Powder. He was raising himself off the ground. She helped him up. There was blood on his forehead. He staggered and she put her arms around him and started to help him back to the tent.

'All right,' said another man. 'We'll go. Just give us time.'

'We'll give you just the time to pack and go,' the farmer said. 'Starting now. Pack and go!'

Derval hadn't woke up, Finn was glad to see. Then he saw Moses coming to the cart, so he got out from under, and silently they got Moe and started to tackle him. When they had done that they tackled the pony and put him under the caravan. Then they roused the children and put them into the cart, and packed up the two tents. There was a light in the caravan and he saw Powder sitting in there and Moses' mother wiping at his forehead with a wet cloth.

It was a menacing situation, working in the light of the torches. They couldn't see the faces of the men that held them. They were just figures, but there were a lot of them, and Finn had no doubt that they meant what they said.

They were the first family to move out. Moses led the pony and Finn led the donkey.

They came to the line of torches and a lane opened for them to go through. Finn kept his head down as they passed through them. Not that it mattered, but he was afraid of the violence he could almost smell. He could see the trouser legs pushed into rubber boots, and the ends of sticks, stout sticks resting on some of the boots. The only thing he could hear was the faint sizzling of the torches, and the awful smell of them.

Then they were past them and the air was clean again, and the road wound and they were free into the fresh air, and his heart stopped pounding. There was no moon, but the sky was filled with stars, and after a time he could discern the sides of the road and the back of the caravan in front of him. They were travelling about a mile when the caravan ahead left

111

the main road and turned down into a side road. It was a much narrower road and it came to an end at the edge of a small lake. There they stopped.

Moses came back to him.

'Don't untackle Moe,' he said to Finn. 'Help me to set up the camps and I'll tell you what to do then.'

Finn helped him. They set up the two tents, and they put the children into their own tent, and Moses lighted a fire. Then he went into the caravan. He came out and said, 'He's all right.' Then he looked at Finn and said, 'You cannot stay, Joseph.' He put Derval into the cart. She was half asleep and half awake. 'Come on,' he said then.

He turned Moe's head, and set off back the way they had come. When he was out of sight of the camp he got up on the cart.

'Up you get now too, Joseph,' he said. 'We have a long way to go before the morning.'

'Why, Moses, why?' Finn asked, bewildered.

Moses hit Moe and he set off at a smart canter.

'Powder was going to sell ye,' said Moses.

Chapter Fourteen

They didn't talk again until the cart came on to the main road. They could just distinguish the hedges at the side of the road. Finn felt it was just as well they couldn't see each other's face. He was holding Derval against him. They were jogging up and down with the movement of the cart.

'Why, Moses?' Finn asked.

'Ach, he knew that Terry was a girl,' he said, 'and he heard about the two kids that there was a reward for. Everybody knows.'

'Did you know?' Finn asked.

'I did,' said Moses. 'When I saw old Moe butting her I knew she was girl. But it didn't matter.'

'Why are you doing this now?' Finn asked.

'Ah, it doesn't matter,' said Moses. 'Powder is not bad, you know. It's just that he thinks a hundred pounds is a lot of money.'

'Don't you think it's a lot of money?' Finn asked.

'Ach, that's different,' said Moses. 'It's not worth selling ye for, I think. But Powder is not bad.'

'He was good to us,' said Finn. 'Didn't he give us shelter and food?'

'That's what I mean,' said Moses. 'You can't blame him. Mebbe, he says, ye'd be better off with the people ye ran from. He sees it that way.'

'What will you do now?' Finn said.

'I'll drop ye miles away,' said Moses. 'Then I'll get

113

back before morning, and when Powder wakes up I'll say ye must have lit out in the night.'

'What will he say?' Finn asked.

'Ach, he'll give me a clout or two,' said Moses. 'But it'll be all right.'

After a while, Finn said: 'If it was for no other reason than I met you, Moses, I'm glad we ran away.'

'Ach, sugar!' said Moses.

'Honest to God,' said Finn.

'Don't be soft,' said Moses. 'Sure, being soft is no good. It's like being clean.'

Finn didn't say any more.

There was a band of light at the end of the eastern sky when Moses pulled up Moe.

'Now,' he said. 'I'll leave ye here. I'll have to go back.'

Finn got down from the cart. He lifted Derval down too, and the bags and clothes.

'There's a town there ahead of ye,' said Moses. 'Skip it. Take the road straight across from ye. Powder will tell the police. He'll hope anyhow. So they will be watching. Get on to the little roads. Get dirty see. Say you are going to the camp. There's always a camp somewhere. They won't bother ye if they think you're tinkers' children.'

'I hope we'll see you again some time, Moses,' said Finn.

'Ach, turnips,' said Moses, pulling Moe's head around to get him facing back the way they had come.

As he swung round Moe spotted the dark figure of Derval and he butted her.

'Oh!' said Derval.

'See,' said Moses, laughing. 'He never done it to a boy.'

Finn swept her out of the way. He patted Moe's head.

'Goodbye, Moe,' he said.

'I'll see ye,' said Moses, then he frightened Moe, shouting, 'Ah! Ah! Ah!' in a loud voice. They could see him for a few seconds waving his arm in the air, and then he was swallowed in the darkness.

'Goodbye, Moses!' Finn called after him. They stood there listening until they could no longer hear the sound of the cart.

'Moses is nice,' said Derval.

'That's right,' said Finn.

'Will he come and see us at Granny's?' Derval asked.

'I hope so,' said Finn. 'I sincerely hope so.'

He sighed, hefted the bags, caught her hand and said, 'Well, we are on our own again, Derval. Start walking.'

Chapter Fifteen

They travelled for two days, and Finn thought he had become as sensitive as an animal. They were lucky with the weather. It seemed to rain mostly at night, and in the daytime the sun shone. They were real April showers, when they came in the day. On a long road he and Derval would walk from a wet patch into a patch where there was no rain at all.

At the sound or sight of a car or a person he had become adept at finding a laneway to turn into, or a hedge to hide in like the little wrens.

At night they would go into one of the haysheds that were behind nearly every farmhouse. Most of the hay was gone after the winter, so there was always a low ledge of hay they could climb up on and sleep. He seemed always to awake before the dawn and they would be on their way to find a hidden place where they could eat. Mainly bread and chocolate, and milk when they could get it. His money was running very low, and he would have become more afraid if they hadn't seen the mountains.

All the land was low, but sometimes when they topped a rise and looked west they could see the blue mountains in the far distance. This encouraged them. He would say to Derval, 'See the mountains way back. Now we can see them. That means that we are coming closer.'

He didn't wash any more after breakfast, remembering what Moses told him. And it worked. They only got a first glance from people, who saw their now-tattered clothes and grimy hands and faces. Finn determined that he would beg if he had to, now that he had learned the art from Moses. He was much bolder going into a shop in a small street town to buy what they wanted.

It was on the third day in the morning that they met the funny man. They were walking through this small town that had a ruined castle near the edge of it, when they passed this man. At first, Finn didn't notice him at all. They just passed and then they heard his voice calling. 'Hey, kid, kid!' Finn was sorry he turned, but it was instinctive with him. He saw the man was very big. He was dressed in a grey suit and wore a wide-brimmed hat, and he had a scar on his face. He came towards them. He was looking closely at Finn. Finn put on the vacant face that Moses had showed him, blank eyes and mouth slightly open.

'Hah?' he said, just like Moses.

'I'm looking for two kids,' this man said. 'I want to tell them something good.'

'Hah?' said Finn again.

The man was screwing up his eyes looking at them. He examined them from head to toe.

'Where do you come from?' the man asked.

'Camp, out the road,' said Finn pointing vaguely with his finger.

'Oh,' the man said, doubtfully. 'You see those kids tell them Nicko wants to see them, eh?'

'Wha' kids?' Finn asked.

The man tightened his mouth. For some reason, Finn was suddenly afraid of him.

'Never mind,' the man said and turned away.

As soon as he had turned away, Finn immediately sought a back lane and turned into it. By this time he knew the value of back lanes. He could almost see the man going over in his mind the things he had noticed about them, and Finn suddenly felt that he would come after them.

The lane wasn't long. It had quite a few rickety wooden doors with latches on them that led into the yards at the back. He knew them well now. Most of the small shops and houses in the country places had these yards where they kept a few pigs and maybe a cow or two and certainly their turf in a shed.

He opened one of these and went in and closed it after him. There was a slit in one of the boards and he put his eye to this.

He was right. He heard the careful footsteps, and he saw the man passing the lane. He was trying the latches of the doors. He came to the one Finn was at. Finn took away his eye and leaned his whole weight against the door. He heard the latch lifting and felt the pressure against his back. He felt this pressure twice and then the latch was put back. He hoped the man thought that the bolt was on the door. His heart was beating fast.

'What is it?' Derval asked, looking at him.

'Shish,' he said, and listened.

He put his eye to the crack again. He heard the footsteps coming back. He saw the man returning, holding his lower lip with his finger and thumb. Then he was past and Finn relaxed. He looked around the yard. The wall at the end was not very high. The stones were white-washed. He went down there and

118

managed to climb up and look over it. There was a muddy lane outside.

'Come on,' he said to Derval, and hoisted her to the top of it. Then he climbed up himself, jumped down and held out his arms for her. She landed safely and he set off at a run along this lane. It went on and on until it came out on the far side of the town on to the main road.

He peeped from behind the hedge here. The road was free on either side except, he saw, for a very old sort of van at the side of the road. It was once a motor car. The back of it had been cut off and a stumpy sort of wooden carry-all had been put there. The man was blowing up a tyre with a hand-pump. He was a thin man who needed a shave but he reminded Finn of Mickser. There was a lot of junk in the back of the van.

Cautiously Finn approached him.

'Can I help you?' he asked.

The man looked up at him.

'You'd save my life if you would, son,' he said. 'I'm running out of wind. I'm like a slack tube.'

Finn took the pump. It was a big cumbersome brass one. The tyre was half inflated. He started to pump.

'God be with the horse,' the man said, wiping his forehead with a piece of rag. 'Put shoes on his hooves, and there you were. No petrol. No machinery. Nothing to go wrong that a dose of castor oil would not cure. Good man, there's great power in you, God bless you.'

Finn kept pumping.

'What has ye on the road?' he asked then. 'Are ye far from yer people?'

119

'They are in the big town on the sea,' said Finn, between pumps.

'Ah, Galway,' he said. 'That's where ye are for, then. Are yer people camped in there?'

'Yes,' said Finn, thinking that's no lie, everybody is people.

'I'm going there,' the man said. 'Sure I'll give ye a lift.'

He lighted a pipe for himself, leaning against the mud-guard.

'I suppose a horse strayed on ye,' he said.

'He did, the divil,' said Finn, imitating Moses.

Derval laughed.

'It's a long walk for the little brother,' the man said.

'Ach, he's tough,' said Finn.

'Ye didn't find him,' the man said.

'No, the divil,' said Finn. 'Maybe we'll see him on the way now.'

'You could do,' the man said. 'They're the divil. All the same they are better than motor cars. Give me a horse any day to a motor car. But times change, eh?'

The tyre was pumped.

'God bless you,' the man said, giving it a kick, 'that should hold us as far as the town. It was lucky for me ye came, and I was lucky for ye. We'll climb on her now and may the divil scald her.'

They got into the front with him. It was very like Mickser's van with all it lacked, but Finn was very glad to be in it. He thought of how lucky they were. They were practically on the last stretch now.

The motor started easily enough, with a few jerks. It wouldn't win a motor race but it would get there, he thought.

'Petrol, oil, bolts, bits and pieces,' the man said.

'No wonder they are under a curse. Wouldn't you want a monkey to pick up all the nuts?' He laughed at this joke, a wheezy laugh.

Finn felt safe with him. He wasn't asking any more questions.

They were a few miles from the town, when this car passed them. It was an odd-coloured car, a sort of pink, the colour that was known as salmon pink, and when it had gone by, Finn thought he recognized the huge back of the man that was driving it

'Get down,' he said to Derval, pushing her off the seat. He got off the seat himself and crouched down.

'What's up with ye?' the man asked in amazement.

'That car,' said Finn, 'the pink one. If he comes back we don't want him to see us.'

'Ah, that one,' the man said. 'I'll tell ye if he comes back. What did ye do to him, tell me? Gave him the wrong change from a five pound note?' He laughed wheezily at this. 'Or is he chasing ye to make ye go to school or what? Eh?'

'I don't know,' said Finn.

'It doesn't matter,' said the man. 'Well, he's coming back I can tell you that. He's backing up the road there. Aren't you a cute young divil? He's straightened out now. He is on his way. Goin' dead slow too. Flatten yeerselves out.' He started to whistle a tune.

Finn could hear the sound of the car even above the engine-sound of this old crock.

'Here he is,' the man said. 'His eyes is like periscopes.' He managed to speak without moving his lips at all hardly. 'He's lookin' at me as if I was his long-lost uncle. Man, he's an ugly lookin' divil. A scar on his face, is that the one?'

'That's him,' said Finn.

121

'Well, he's past now,' the man said, 'but don't get up. I bet he'll turn behind and pass us again. Wait'll you see.' He looked into the cracked driving mirror in front of him. 'There he is! What did I tell you? Don't move.'

They stayed where they were.

'He's comin' now, blastin' the road,' he said. 'He'll leave us smothered in dust. There he goes now. He is looking in his mirror, I'd say. Well, what did he see? Nothin'. He's as wise now as ever he will be. Ye can get up now. He's out of sight.'

Finn cautiously raised his head and looked. The road was clear in front of them. 'All right,' he said to Derval, and they sat up on the seat.

'What was all that about now?' the man asked. 'No! Don't tell me. I like mysteries, see. I can be makin' up stories about it for the rest of time. If I knew, there'd be no fun in it. When I don't know, I can make all sorts of tales about it. Isn't this better?'

'I don't know.' said Finn.

'I do,' he said. 'Most stories has no mysteries in them. It's just nothing when you hear the truth. Sometimes lies is better than truth for the sake of adventure.'

Finn was thinking. That car, with its odd pink colour. He had seen it once or twice before today, when they had pulled back into the shelter of a hedge or a by-way. He couldn't puzzle it out. Who was the man? He didn't look like police. It couldn't be a man that Uncle Toby had hired to find them apart from the police, or could it? Whoever he was, Finn was afraid of him, and he decided that whenever they saw a pink-coloured car they would run.

The man dropped them a mile from the town. Finn

waved his hand at some tinkers' caravans that were parked near a wood. He thanked the man gruffly. The man let them down, waved cheerfully at them, and while he was in sight, Finn and Derval walked towards the caravans.

Then Finn altered course, and walked on the traffic-filled road for a time, before he sought the shelter of anonymous side roads. Eventually he found a sort of footpath that went beside the railway. They walked on this, cautiously, a long way and crossed a bridge over a wide stretch of water, climbed a hill and came into a sort of square where many buses were lined up, nose to tail, outside stone steps leading up to the railway station. He knew this was it. There were many people on the path near the station, and he thought it might be safe to walk down there.

He thought so until he saw the uniforms of the police. There were many of them, and they were looking at all the passengers that were getting on the buses. Finn pulled back, his heart sinking.

Chapter Sixteen

Finn was wondering how they could get out of the square under the eyes of the police. He didn't like to think that they would have to turn around and go back the way they had come.

Suddenly almost under his eyes a lot of men in slightly gaudy uniforms started to get into ranks. They all had brass instruments and one man had a huge drum. He gave this a few bangs, the men formed and started to play a rousing tune, and moved off in step. The effect was like that created by the Pied Piper of Hamelin. One moment there was nobody but the band and buses and police and people, and in the next few minutes there were literally hundreds of children, of all sorts and sizes. Finn couldn't believe his eyes as he saw them surrounding the band on all sides, calling and screaming and hurrooing and marching in step with them.

'Quick,' he said to Derval, grabbed her hand and ran after the band and started to elbow his way in amongst all the children.

You would think that it was all laid on especially for himself and Derval. He raised an arm and cried 'Hurrah!' It was terrific. Boom-boom-boom and Blah-blah-blah. The music was exciting and the screaming of the children was exciting, so much so that as they passed the buses, he almost forgot to look at the destination names on the front of them. He saw

Carraigmore and his heart leaped. Despite them all, he thought, we have come to the end of the railway line. He saw that the driver was in the cabin of the bus, with the window lowered looking out and laughing as the band and the children passed. Finn kept his eye on the bus, and before they got too far away, he saw it turning out of the line and slowly following after.

Down the band went through the town, booming, startling the people who were going about. They would stop and stare and laugh. It put them in good humour.

If Finn had asked for it, he couldn't have got it so good. His only worry was the bus, and he kept looking over his shoulder. Somewhere the band turned to the right, and he prayed that the bus would be going that direction too. He was in agony until he saw that it turned right too, so he got back to enjoying the music and the screaming and singing of the children.

On and on they went, down a street and another turn to the left and on and over a bridge that had small pillars instead of walls, and on and on and over another bridge up a long road with a wall on the right and at the top of this place the band and the children swung left and as he watched the bus, he saw that it was going to turn to the right, so grabbing Derval's hand he started to ease his way through the crowd over to the right, and soon he was free of them and watching the back of the bus going away and away from them, but he didn't mind now. They hadn't the money to pay for seats anyhow, but the principal thing was that he knew the direction it was going and he could follow after it.

They walked quite a long way before they were

clear of houses, but now it had started to rain, and people were so busy rushing by under umbrellas, or fixing plastic raincoats or headgear on themselves that two dirty-looking, drenched children meant very little to any of them.

They had come to the place where footpaths ended and they were walking on the road when this car pulled up beside them. It wasn't a new car, and it wasn't an old car, and principally it wasn't a pink car.

This lady opened the car door and shouted at them.

'Come in for heaven's sake, come in out of the rain!'

Finn looked at her. She was dressed in tweed clothes. She wasn't a young lady. She wore a man's sort of tweed hat with a red feather in it.

'Where are you heading for?' she asked impatiently.

Finn let his mouth go slack and pointed ahead of them.

'All right, get in, get in!' she said. 'I cannot stay here all day. Come on!'

He took the decision and moved over to the open car door. He made Derval go ahead of him and he got in after her and closed the door.

'Now,' the lady said. 'It's not a nice day for children like you to be walking the roads. Where are your people?'

'Back, back,' said Finn pointing ahead of him.

'Why are you straying?' she asked.

'Town,' said Finn. 'Messages. Follow after.'

'You mean they moved on and left you to follow?' She was outraged. 'This is not good. You will get your death of cold. People have to be free, I know, but they don't have to be uncivilized. I'll take you as far as I go. When you see your people let me know and I'll give them a piece of my mind.'

Finn was sorry already for his mythical people.

It was nice in the car. Sheets of rain were coming down. It was nice to be sheltered from it, and every turn of the wheels was bringing them closer and closer to their destination.

'And the way you people treat your dogs,' the lady said, 'and the dear little donkeys. It's disgraceful. Don't they teach you to be nice to animals?'

'Yes, ma'am,' said Finn.

The clouds were dark and heavy, but over to the right there were patches of blue in the sky and they made the lakes there look blue too, and inviting.

'They let the hooves of the donkeys grow disgracefully,' she said. 'How the poor things must suffer.'

Finn wasn't listening to her now, because he had looked in the mirror and there behind them, staying at an even distance was a pink-coloured car.

Finn was startled. He stared straight ahead of them. The lady kept on talking, but he hardly heard what she said. He looked behind again. There were two other cars between them and the pink car now. He hoped it wasn't the same car but he had a terrible feeling that it was.

Also when they turned the next corner, the lady had to slow the car because there was a line of cars stopped in front of her. At the head of the line was a bus. Finn was positive that it was the Carraigmore bus. He saw a policeman coming out of it and waving the bus on. As it started off the policeman went to the next car and spoke to the driver. Finn saw that there were other policemen, examining the people in the other cars too.

He caught Derval's hand and opened the car door. 'We have to go now, ma'am,' he said, 'the camp is just down the road.'

'But—' she protested.

He gave her no more time.

'Thank you, ma'am,' he said. They got out of the car fast. He looked behind and saw the roof of the pink car behind the other two cars. He saw the opening of a road on the right, and going behind the lady's car he walked into it and then started to run.

Will we be always running, he wondered. It was a winding lane, but it was wide enough for a car. There were no hedges each side of it but loose stone walls. He didn't think the police had seen them, but he wondered about the man in the pink car. Also he wondered if the lady would tell the police that she had two dirty children in the car with her. It is too bad, he thought. We were so near, so near. His immediate worry was the pink car, so as he ran, he tried to listen.

He was near an iron gate when he thought he heard the sound of an engine. He tried the gate. It wasn't locked, so he opened it and went in and closed it behind him. A run of a few yards brought them to a clump of bushes and tangled briars. Beyond that was a mound and on top of the mound was an old castle. It was a square castle, rising from its buttressed base. He ran towards it. He didn't know why. He was a bit confused. They crossed a dike where a moat had one time been, and then he saw the square opening into the castle and he went in. The bottom place was littered with the droppings of cattle, and to the left he saw steps. He went towards them. They were narrow stone steps set in the side of the castle tower, winding to the top. They were well preserved except for the first ones. He went up and up, holding to the side of the rounded walls.

'Finn,' said Derval, 'I'm afraid.'

'No, Derval,' he said. 'When we get to the top we'll be able to see.' That must be the reason, he thought. The castle was built on a height, and if he got to the top he would be able to see all around. This seemed to him a good thing then.

He wondered how far the steps went. There was an arch on the first floor. He looked in there, and looked up and could see the sky above his head where the castle reared.

He continued on, second floor, third floor, and then fourth floor. There was a three-foot ledge of flagstones here, all round the top. One time, hundreds of years ago, it had been part of the roof of the castle, where sentinels walked perhaps. He looked down. There was a fifty-foot fall to the bottom. No floors left, only the ledges and holes cut in the stone where the floor tresses had been laid. You could see one or two stone fireplaces sticking incongruously in the walls.

He stepped on to the flags and looked over the top.

He could see the mountains and the big lake on his left, and rivers and streams and the smoke rising from the chimneys of the village quite a short distance away.

He ducked down and pulled Derval with him when he saw the pink car pulled up outside the gate.

'What is it, Finn?' she asked. 'What is it?'

'Nothing, Derval,' he said. 'Just keep down. Don't make a sound.'

I made a mistake, he thought. I should never have

129

come into this beckoning castle. We should have taken to the fields. We could have hidden ourselves behind the walls or in the briars. There were thousands of hiding places, and I had to pick the castle. Solid, hundreds of years old. If you listened you might hear the laughter of men, and the clashing of shields and swords. See helmets glinting in the sunlight. But now all he was listening for was the sound of footsteps.

And his heart sank when he heard them.

First scuffling, and then the sound of leather on the stone steps. Why should I be so afraid, he wondered. This Nicko is only a man. What harm could there be in him? He could have told the police about them and they would have been caught days ago. Why didn't he? It was this ignorance about him that made Finn afraid.

It was a terrible situation to be in. They couldn't run any more. They couldn't go over and climb down the steep sides of the castle. They couldn't run down the steps into the arms of the man, if it was he. Why did he come into the castle? It was the last place he should have come. The rain had stopped. There were still some pools of water on the flags. It would be easy to slip on them and fall down to the cold dung-covered floor at the bottom.

Then the opening was filled with this man.

He had to bend his head to come through.

He looked at the two children crouched against the wall. He held out his hand.

'Don't be frightened,' he said. 'I'm your friend.'

Finn didn't think so. The hand he held out was shaking and his face was absolutely wet with sweat. Finn rose to his feet, putting Derval behind him.

130

'We read about you, about your flight. You are Finn aren't you, and this is your sister, Derval?'

Finn didn't answer him.

'Look,' he said. 'Your uncle was worried about you.'

'Uncle Toby is not worried about us,' said Finn.

'I don't mean him,' said Nicko. 'I'm talking about your Uncle Gerry in America. He sent me all the way to find you. He wants to look after you. He doesn't like the way you were treated.'

He moved another step towards them.

They moved away from him. Finn reached his hand out to the broken wall and found a stone that fitted his fist.

'Don't be like that, kid,' Nicko said. 'It will be all right, I tell you. Come with me. We'll have a good time. You'll see a new land and you'll have fun.'

They backed away from him.

He didn't want to look at it, but he knew the flags were broken behind them, that they had only another few paces to go and they would fall. He hoped he didn't have to put his hands on them. If they fell on their own, that would be an accident, wouldn't it?

Finn knew this too. He raised the stone.

'Keep away from us,' he said. Derval was gripping him around the hips, her head hidden in his back.

At this moment he heard a call coming from below. He thought at first he was dreaming, but he heard it again.

'Finn! Finn!' this voice was calling.

He dared to turn his head, and there below, waving up at him, was the man Michael, still calling his name.

He felt his limbs shaking as he waved his hand.

'Oh, Michael! Michael!' he called. 'Come here! Come here!' and it was only then he turned to look at Nicko who was leaning back against the wall and wiping his face with a handkerchief.

Chapter Seventeen

Even at that distance, the sight of Finn's face, grimy, sunburned and yet pale with fright sent Michael up the stairs of the castle as if he was trying to break a record.

He had to stop at the final entrance to catch his breath. This big fellow was in the corner with a handkerchief in his hand, but the folds of fat on the back of his neck were wet with sweat.

Finn was looking at him, Michael, as if he was an unexpected Christmas box. Derval was peeping out from behind her brother, and her face, too, was pale.

'Hello, Finn. Hello, Derval,' he said. 'I have been looking for you. I'm glad I found you. Are you coming?'

Finn looked at the stone in his hand, and then let it fall. He watched until it bounced on the floor below. Then he caught Derval's hand and walked past Nicko. He was glad to see that Michael was nearly as big as Nicko.

Derval held out her arms. Michael bent and lifted her, and she put her face into his neck. He was affected by this. He thought of their wanderings since he had left them. He was sorry he hadn't done something more definite.

'We'll go down,' he said, and carried her to the bottom.

In the field outside he left her down. She kept

133

holding his hand. He looked at them. Derval, like Finn, needed to be washed.

'What happened?' he asked.

'That man,' said Finn. 'He talked funny. I don't know what he meant. He frightened us.'

'Fright is over now,' said Michael. 'I have been coming up against this pink car cutting across your trail as I followed you. Do you know you are not far from home?'

'How far?' Finn asked.

Michael walked with them to the gate.

He was upset about the fellow in the car himself. He couldn't place him; didn't know why he was around.

'Go back the way you came from,' he said. 'When you come to the main road turn third on the left. This is a little road that will ring the village for you. Then you will come on another road that goes towards the hill. Follow this. When you come to the top of it you will look down and see the sea. Carraigmore is at the foot of it.'

'Where will you be?' Derval asked.

'I will be talking to this man,' said Michael. 'I have a bicycle and I will be behind you. I will catch up with you. You mustn't be frightened any more. You understand that?'

'Yes,' said Finn.

'You have a good brother there, Derval,' he said to her. 'You stick with him and you'll be all right.'

'Yes,' said Derval.

'Get going now,' he said. 'In two hours you should be home.'

They nodded. There was a little more colour in Finn's face. They were soon gone around the bend in

134

the road. Michael looked at the pink car. He opened the door, saw the keys were in the ignition, took them out, tossed them in his hand and sat on the stone wall.

He had gone across the sea. He had met the Inspector. Together they had visited all the neighbours of Uncle Toby. They had learned a lot. Before he left home Uncle Toby had talked a little, in his cups. It was a clue to what Michael needed. It provided a motive for the pursuit of the two children, but Uncle Toby's employer, the solicitor, had been tight-lipped and uncommunicative. They had cabled to America, with the feeble information they had. They didn't know enough. Was this man part of it? What was it about? How could he have made Finn so afraid?

He watched Nicko coming out towards the gate.

He was a big man, Michael saw. If he had to tangle with him, he would need all the tricks he knew. Thinking of the look on Finn's face, and Derval snuggling her face into his neck, he thought: Why, I would kill him if I had to.

Nicko came out, closed the gate. He stood in front of Michael. He was really a very big man. Michael thought he might have been a wrestler. He stood there looking at Michael, who noticed that his eyes were almost unblinking.

'Who are you?' Nicko asked.

'Who are you?' asked Michael. 'You frightened those children.'

'That's not so,' Nicko said.

'Why are you here?' Michael asked.

'Mind your own business,' Nicko said. He walked to the car and got into it. Then as he went to turn the key, he saw that it was gone. He came out of the car again. Michael was tossing the keys in his hand.

'If you want them you will have to take them, won't you?' he said.

'Look, I want no trouble from you,' Nicko said.

Michael stood up, put the keys in his pocket.

'I will give you the keys,' he said, 'when you answer some questions.'

He thought Nicko was going to attack him. He tensed his muscles, waiting. I mustn't let him get too close to me, he thought.

'I'm a friend of their uncle Gerry,' Nicko said. 'We read about those brave kids in the papers. "I have a better right to mind those kids than this Toby," Gerry said. "We must help those kids." "Take a gamble," we says, like good horse racers. We make a collection and I was sent over to help the kids. That's it.'

It all seemed crazy now, the whole idea, like a nightmare dreamed up in dimly lighted clubs and saloons by men in terrible need of money. Their whole life was a gamble and this had been just another one, that might have come in at even money. Spend a little to make a little.

'I don't like it,' said Michael.

'You don't have to like it,' said Nicko.

'Why were they frightened?' Michael asked.

Nicko wiped sweat off his forehead again. He didn't like to think of the moment in the castle. It was a temptation. If the kids had an accident then the legacy would belong to Gerry instead of all this trouble of finding them and trying to bring them out so that Gerry could mind them and draw from the funds as their guardian.

'I was the wrong one to send,' he said. 'I don't look

136

like Father Christmas. The kids wouldn't listen to me. I would have helped them good. I'll take the keys now.'

'You won't take these keys for half an hour,' said Michael. 'We will just sit here for half an hour, and then I'll give you the keys.' He waited for a reaction. He thought at first Nicko would jump him. He didn't. He sat on the wall opposite to Michael, and took out a cheroot and lighted it from a gold lighter.

'Who are you?' Nicko asked.

Now Michael was in a dilemma. What could he say? 'I am a policeman'? Then Nicko could say, 'Well, why didn't you grab the kids?' So he couldn't say he was a policeman. So he couldn't back himself with the authority of the policeman. So far as this man was concerned, Michael was a civilian like anyone else.

'I'm nobody much,' said Michael. 'I'm just keeping an eye on these children. We will give them half an hour to go where they are going, then I will give you the keys. After that you will go, and if you take my advice you will go south and not west.'

'Who says?' Nicko asked. 'It's just because I'm a decent man that I don't grind you into dust. I don't want trouble, is why. Nobody has any right to hold a person like this. I'm just playing along with you. I'll give you the half-hour, but after that you are in trouble.'

'You will go south,' said Michael, 'not west, or I assure you that you will walk into lots and lots of trouble.'

That was all they said.

It was a long half-hour. Michael in his mind's eye could see the children out of the village, walking down the mountain road, coming to the top of it and looking down on the sea and the thatched cottages looking like tiny doll's-houses way below.

When the time was up he gave the man the keys and watched him drive off, got his bicycle from the side of the road, mounted it and cycled casually up the lane, not realizing that he was a fool.

For Nicko had overheard the instructions he had given the children, and Nicko did not know that he was a policeman. On reaching the main road Nicko paused and thought: Why should I do what this fellow says? Who is he? He imagined having to tell Gerry and the boys how he had failed to persuade the children to come with him. When he had his hands so nearly on them. They would expect him to have put up a better fight for Gerry's rights. So the pink car turned not south but west and took the turning third on the left.

Michael cycled in a leisurely fashion through the village and turned left towards the foothills. He cycled up the long winding road against the rise of the hill, congratulating himself that he was in good condition to be able to do this.

But when he got to the top of the pass that looked down on the coast below, he couldn't see a thing. A heavy mist had come in from the sea and covered the whole mountain plain and halfway down its sides and was increasing in density.

Then he saw the pink car pulled into a cutting off the road. He could hardly believe his eyes. He got off the bicycle and looked at it. The keys were in the ignition. He will never learn, Michael thought. He climbed up the steep side of the gully and looked around him. The great bog plain stretched away from him, but he couldn't see more than a yard in front of him.

The children would have seen the pink car. They would have left the road and Nicko stopped the car and took off after them.

Oh, you fool, Michael, he told himself. For a few moments he was in a panic. He wanted to rush off into the mist on the mountains calling their names. He knew that wouldn't do any good. He knew that the mountains were dangerous in a mist. They were filled with soft patches that could swallow an elephant if he walked into them. Bogholes, outcrops, sudden falls, a treacherous, dangerous place to be in a fog like this. Bad enough with all that, but Nicko as well.

Now Michael found himself sweating. He deliberately sat down and thought about the situation. He forced the panic out of his thoughts.

Then he rose and he went to the car, got in, turned it and set off back down to the village.

He startled the Sergeant.

'How many men have you?' he asked, showing his identification at the same time.

'Only four.'

'Right, get ten of the men of the village, and come with me. Those Dove kids are wandering on the mountain and the mist is down. We'll set out a long line of men. We will have to find them.'

While the Sergeant got organized, Michael got on the telephone. He was sorry he had to cut short his holidays. He was sorry that they would have to find the children. He wondered sadly what Finn and Derval would think when they found out he was a policeman. Would they think that he had betrayed them? It couldn't be helped. The situation was too serious.

It was even more serious than he had thought when the message came through, all about the legacy, and an uncle over there who benefited if the children died. He felt cold chills on his neck thinking of the man in the pink car. He wouldn't do a thing like that. Wouldn't he? If he was desperate enough? He wasn't their uncle. Suppose the children had fallen in the castle. That would have been an accident, wouldn't it? Suppose they drowned in a boghole, that would be an accident, wouldn't it? Who could prove any different?

'Sergeant, hurry, hurry, for the love of God,' Michael called.

In half an hour a long line of men, fifty yards between each man, walked into the dense mist, and kept in touch by calling, calling the names of two children.

Chapter Eighteen

Finn saw Carraigmore from the top of the mountain road.

It lay below at his feet. The sky was misting over, but a shaft of sunlight seemed to pinpoint it for his eye.

'Look! Look!' he said to Derval.

He could even pick out Granny O'Flaherty's house from his memory now, the white cottage close to the sea with the whitewashed stone wall surrounding it. Memories came flooding back to him as if the pages of his diary had come alive.

He had little time to savour it, for suddenly he heard the sound of a car coming from behind, and when he looked he could hardly believe his eyes. But it was the pink car and it was coming fast. This was like dreaming a nightmare several times over. What had happened to Michael, he wondered?

He didn't hesitate.

'Come on,' he said to Derval. He seemed to be always saying, 'Come on!' to Derval. They left the road, climbed the tall bank and were free on the side of the mountain, and they started to run towards the distant sea.

It wasn't easy. The ground was deceptive. Parts of it were very hard near outcrops of rock. Other parts where turf had been cut from the deep sections were very soft. Other parts where the mountain streams had cut gashes in the side were steep and rock-strewn and many sheep had been killed falling into them. Why, he had been on this mountain many times before, he remembered now, with the pony and Uncle Paddy. That's right. If it wasn't Uncle Paddy, it was Uncle Joe. They had sheep on the mountain and Finn had been here whole days with the sheepdog when they were rounding up the sheep to bring them below and dip them, or bringing up the donkey with the panniers to collect baskets of the dried turf.

And they were running downhill. This made it easier.

He stopped and turned.

There was Nicko coming after them, running for all he was worth. Suddenly all the fear left Finn as he watched him. It was obviously the first time that Nicko had ever been on the side of a coarse mountain. He didn't know the difference between the soft places and the hard places. He was floundering. He was wearing light shoes. They were already wet. Once his leg had gone into a soft part up to the knee. Finn could see the brown bog mud on his light grey suit.

'Hey, kid! Kid!' Nicko called. 'I don't mean any harm, I tell you. I wouldn't do nothing to you. Hear this.'

Finn caught Derval's hand and ran on with her. He had to choose his places, but he knew where he was going. Unfortunately, Derval did not. She was slowing him down. She was slowing him more than the awkwardness of Nicko.

He bent down. 'Get up on my back,' he said to Derval. She obeyed him immediately. He marvelled at the way she had obeyed him all the time. She got up on his back. He didn't hurry. Out of the corner of one eye he watched the approach of Nicko, and with the other he saw in amazement that a great mist was closing in on them from the top of the mountain, and also sweeping in from below and the sides.

When he saw that Nicko wasn't ten yards away, he started to run again with Derval on his back.

He had chosen his place carefully before the mist came down. He had spotted this section of about twenty square yards that looked as green and inviting as a field. But he knew from the look of it that it wasn't any such thing. He knew this, but Nicko wouldn't know it. He slowed his pace until Nicko was almost on his heels and then he ran across it. The idea was to put your foot on a part that was brown and keep away from the green. Because the green wasn't grass but moss that looked like grass. He jumped from brown bit to brown bit, and he didn't stop or lose his concentration until he was clear of it and found hard ground under his feet. Then he left Derval on the ground and turned to look.

Nicko was really floundering. He was up to his armpits in the green slime and was clutching around him, and shouting, 'Here! Here! Here!' Finn saw the panic in his face. Well, he thought, he made us afraid and now he is afraid.

'Wait here,' he said to Derval. He went over to the left where he had seen a bank that turf had been cut from. Here there was a four-foot length of tree that had been buried in the bog for hundreds of years until it had been dug out by the turfcutters. It had lain in the sun for years, so it was quite light now. He bent under this and raised it in his arms and staggered

143

back to the place where Nicko was sinking into the mire.

He paused at the edge and threw it so that it landed in front of the man. It splashed his face. Some of the stuff went into his open mouth. He spat it out.

'Hold on to that,' said Finn. Nicko wrapped his arms around it, as if it was a lifebelt, which indeed it was.

'You can work your way out with that,' Finn said, and then turned away.

'Don't go, kid. Hey, kid! Don't go!' Nicko called, but already Finn was out of his sight, for the mountain mist had closed over them.

Finn found Derval just in time too.

Then he stood there, Nicko's voice in his ears. They couldn't see a yard in front of them.

For a moment he felt panic. He tried to remember if there was a wind before the mist, and then remembered that there was a gentle one that was blowing from the sea. He felt it now. He turned until he felt it on his face. So if they headed into the wind, they should be in the right direction.

'Hold tight,' he said to Derval. 'Don't lose me.'

She gripped him tightly, and he set off.

He was making very slow progress. He was afraid of the ground under his feet. It was hard to see. They could easily tumble into a boghole or a crevasse without knowing until it was too late. A group of rocks loomed up in front of them. There was grass around the rocks and a few blackberry briars. He stopped there.

If only the mist would lift, he thought. He could still hear the voice of Nicko, but it seemed farther away. If he was wrong about the wind they could be walking up the mountain instead of down and they wouldn't know.

'I think we'll stay here for a while,' he said to Derval. They sat on the grass. It was like living in an opaque world, a beautiful white world that made you lightheaded. Far away he could hear the bleating of sheep. This was the only sound they heard for some time and then he heard the calling of their names.

'Finn! Derval! Finn! Derval!' Not just one voice but many voices coming from all sides behind them. This was Michael's idea but Finn didn't know it. It was to give comfort and let the children know that people were on hand to help them.

Yes, but what kind of people, Finn wondered, as he choked off a cry he was going to make in return? They could be the police. He didn't think they could be people from Carraigmore, because the voices seemed to be coming from the wrong direction.

He made up his mind.

'We'll have to go,' he said.

He put up his face and moved it until he felt the gentle wind blowing on it, and then he set off at a good pace. When they hit a soft spot and floundered, he pulled back. 'You'll have to get on my back again, Derval,' he said. So she got on his back. He bent under her weight, but this kept his face closer to the ground and he could spot where he was putting his feet, and he didn't have to worry about Derval.

At one stage he came on very hard ground, but it was ridged since the time people had to grow potatoes on the mountainside. There was a whole field of this bounded by loose rocks.

Still it seemed to him that the calling voices were coming closer and closer, and his heart beat faster.

145

After all, he thought, these men would know the mountain better than he did. They would know it by various marks and they could travel it, even in this mist, much faster than he could.

Their voices were definitely closer.

Wouldn't it be terrible at this last minute to be caught for Uncle Toby? It'd make you want to cry, he thought, as he ran on, his breath coming hard in his chest now.

The voices seemed to be enveloping them now. He wondered if he would try and find a place amongst stones where they could hide until the searchers had passed them by and the mountain mist had lifted.

Almost as he thought it, the mist lifted. It was like magic. One second it was there and the next second it was gone and the whole land was revealed basking in the evening sunlight.

He looked behind him in a panic.

There they were, a long line of men stretched out on the mountainside, some of them carrying sticks, wearing rubber boots and among them the uniform of police.

He didn't look any more. He took Derval off his back, caught her hand and started to fly down the mountain.

He heard the shouts behind him.

There were red spots in front of his eyes. He was terribly disappointed. To have come so close and to lose at this last gasp. Oh, no, he thought, don't let them.

'Look! Look!' he heard Derval say. 'Look!'

He blinked and looked. About thirty yards from them two men were coming towards them, but they were riding white ponies, urging them on, shouting.

Finn kept running automatically. The men were laughing. The ponies' tails were flying. The men had just shirts and trousers, and they had no saddles on the ponies. Finn couldn't believe his eyes. They were they! Uncle Paddy and Uncle Joe, big fellows, with their white teeth gleaming, and almost before he knew it, the men and the ponies were beside them, arms scooped and Derval was caught up in front of Uncle Paddy and Finn was swept up in front of Uncle Joe.

See, he thought. I knew it, I knew that Granny O'Flaherty would stretch out her arms.

'Hello, Finn,' said Joe.

'Hello, Derval,' said Paddy.

'Yah-ha-hoo!' shouted Paddy.

'Yah-ha-hoo!' shouted Joe, turning to wave an arm derisively at the closing line of men, and then the ponies started to run down the mountain, leaping stone walls, jumping gullies, as sure-footed as goats, heading for the sea below and the house, and Granny O'Flaherty, a wild, wild ride, so exhilarating that Finn found himself shouting out loud, and behind them Michael watched, and if they could have seen him, waved a hand in benediction and laughed out loud.

Chapter Nineteen

Granny O'Flaherty was waiting for them in front of the house. She was just as Finn had remembered her, a tall woman with a square face and a hooked nose, with black hair going grey in a taut bun at the back of her head, wearing a long red petticoat, men's boots and a grey blouse with a cameo brooch.

When Uncle Joe let him down from the pony he went in to her. She waited for him.

'Hello, Granny,' he said.

She looked at him.

'It took you long enough to get here,' she said.

Finn laughed.

She was the same as ever. She sounded very gruff. But when Uncle Toby was gruff you shivered, and when Granny was gruff you laughed. That was a big difference.

She put her hand on his shoulder. The feel of it was warm.

'Better late than never,' she said. 'I knew you would make it. This house and all we have belong to you.'

'Oh, Granny,' he said, catching her hand.

'Don't go soft now,' she said. 'We haven't time. The game is not over yet.'

'Here's Derval,' said Uncle Paddy, who had carried her in from the pony's back. Derval had a finger in her mouth.

148

'Put her down,' said Granny. He did so. She looked at her. Derval was a bit afraid.

'You are very dirty,' said Granny.

'We had to be dirty,' said Derval. 'Like Moses.'

'And who cut your hair?' Granny asked.

'Finn did,' said Derval, 'with a big knife. I had to be a boy you see. My name was Terry.'

'If only you could see the cut of yourself,' said Granny. 'You are like a trickey.'

'I like being dirty,' said Derval.

'We all like being dirty,' said Granny, 'but we have to think of the neighbours. We are glad to see you Derval.'

'Finn said everything would be all right when we got to you,' said Derval.

'Finn knew what he was talking about,' she said. 'Will you come in now and let me wash you?'

'I suppose so,' said Derval with a sigh.

Granny cackled.

'Joe,' she said, 'go down to the shop and get a dress for her and clothes and shoes and things.'

'How do I know her size?' Joe asked.

'Look at her,' she said.

'Not enough,' said Joe. He took a piece of string from his pocket and knelt in front of Derval, and solemnly measured from her neck to her knee.

'Paddy,' said Granny. 'Loose out the ponies and then come back and keep an eye on the gate. Don't let anybody in. How soon will they be here?'

'Half an hour,' said Paddy.

'Can't I go with him?' said Finn.

'You cannot,' said Granny. 'You want to scrape the dirt off you and change your clothes and keep under cover for a while. Right.'

She took Derval's hand and went into the house. Joe went up the road and Paddy took the ponies. He jumped on the back of one and grabbed the reins of the other, and went racing down the road.

The house was the same as Finn remembered it. A thatched roof of new straw. The open fireplace was filled with a range. The two three-legged stools still stood in front of the range as they had in front of the open fire. Granny went into the back place where there was a bathroom, and Finn let his burdens fall on the floor and sat on a stool. He could feel the warmth coming from the range.

He just let himself go lax. He felt very tired. He leaned back against the wall and let his chin fall on his chest. We did it, he thought, despite everything, we did it. He closed his eyes. He could see black spots dancing.

Then he heard Derval talking. It was a long time since he had heard her talking so much. She was telling Granny everything. She had remembered all the names: Poll and Mickser and Michael and Moses. He noticed that she didn't mention Nicko. She hadn't seen much of him anyhow. She had kept her face hidden any time that he was around. Granny listened to her closely. He heard her say: You didn't! He did! Imagine that! Go away! encouraging the floods of conversation.

Suddenly Finn thought: This is what it is all about. This is why I did it, so that she would be with people who would love her and listen to her talking. Just that, if nothing else.

He must have nodded off to sleep.

He came awake with Granny upbraiding him.

'Sleeping at a time like this,' she was saying, 'when we have to man the trenches.'

150

Derval was as clean as a whistle. She had a towel wrapped around her. Her face was glowing. It didn't harm her anyhow, he thought. He saw even if Granny was fighting him that she was looking at him a bit anxiously, her head on one side.

'In with you,' she said. 'Clean yourself. Throw out the dirty clothes. Do you want to disgrace us?'

Finn grinned and went into the bathroom. It felt very good to lie back in hot water, to clean himself and wash his hair. He thought of Moses. He thought that Moses would like a hot bath if somebody would give it to him.

When he went down with the cleanest clothes he could find on him Derval was dressed in a pink dress and white socks and shiny patent leather shoes. She looked different. It was funny to see big Joe down on his knees, buttoning her dress at the back.

'Amn't I pretty?' Derval was asking.

'How could you be pretty with boy's hair?' Granny was asking.

'It is a pretty dress,' Derval was saying.

Paddy filled the doorway then.

'They are coming down the road now,' he said.

'All right,' said Granny. 'Finn, stay here with Derval. Don't come out whatever happens.'

'All right,' said Finn.

'Will they take us away from you, Granny?' Derval asked.

There was a silence then as they looked at one another.

'I'd like to stay here with you,' said Derval.

Me too, Finn thought.

Granny went on her knees in front of her.

'Nobody is going to take you away from me,' she said. 'You hear that!'

'Oh, I'm glad,' said Derval, throwing her arms around her neck.

Granny was looking at Finn. She smiled at him. She rose and patted Derval's head. 'You belong to us,' she said. 'We won't let you go.'

'Close the door after us,' she said to Finn, and then she and Paddy and Joe went out.

Finn closed the door. He saw there was a bolt. He shot this and then went over to the window. It was a small window with a pot of geraniums on it. He could see out. Derval pulled at his leg, so he got a wooden chair and put it near the window so that she could stand and look out. He put his arm around her. Granny stood at the closed gate, Paddy and Joe one each side of her. Fronting her was a big sergeant, several policemen and the men who had been searching the hill.

'Now, Mrs O'Flaherty,' the Sergeant said. 'We don't want any trouble. These children are the Wards of the Court and we have to take them away.'

'What children?' Granny asked.

'Now, look,' he said. 'We all know you have the children.'

'How do you know?' she asked.

'For God's sake, Mrs O'Flaherty,' he said, 'didn't we see the two lads grabbing them on to the ponies, Paddy and Joe there?'

'How do you know?' she asked.

'Didn't we see them?' he said, getting a bit exasperated.

'You might have seen somebody like them,' she said.

'All right,' he said. 'Just let us go into the house and we can settle it once and for all.'

'Have you a warrant?' she asked.

'What would I be doing with a warrant?' he asked.

'To put your big toe across my threshold,' she said, 'you need a warrant. To shove your big nose past the portals you need a warrant. Tell me if you have one.'

'No, I haven't one,' he said. 'But I can soon get one.'

'Well go away and get it,' she said. 'Because you are not going to pass this gate without it.'

'Now, look here, Mrs O'Flaherty,' he said. 'Let us be sensible.'

'You can be as sensible as you like,' she said.

'You know damn well you can't fight the law like that. Are you setting yourself up against the law of the land? Do that and you know what will happen. Don't you know well you can't win a fight like this?'

'Nobody knows whether they can win a fight until they start it,' she said. 'It has to be started. You start it, and I tell you now that I'll finish it.'

'All right,' he said, 'if you want fight, you'll get it. I'll be back here in the morning with the warrant and authority. I'm warning you. The law is the law and there's no getting around it. It doesn't matter who you are, Granny O'Flaherty or anybody else, they have to abide by the law or suffer the consequences.'

'Away with you!' she said. 'Come back with your warrant. Come back with a regiment of soldiers and all the police in the county. Come back with cannon and machine guns. Do your worst, Sergeant. Nobody is going to take those children from the O'Flahertys.'

She turned her back on him and walked towards the house.

'Now, Mrs O'Flaherty,' he said plaintively after her. She just flicked her hand in the air, and walked in the door that Finn had opened for her.

'Now,' she said, 'we'll eat. The day before the battle, eh, Finn?'

'Will they beat us, Granny?' he asked.

'Let them try,' she said. 'Just let them try.'

Chapter Twenty

Carraigmore looked very well on this sunny morning. There it was, a village of white-washed thatched cottages, built with no definite order, you would think, in small stony fields, leading up to hills that became mountains, and backed in the distance by blue mountains far off, and in front of it the sea with many islands, and long beaches of white sand.

A pretty place, you would say, but a place of no importance.

Well, if it was of no importance, an awful lot of people were taking a great interest in it. There were cars coming from all directions, and men with cameras were debouching and setting things up. There were all kinds of cameras, tripod ones and flash ones, and ciné-cameras. There were men up on the telephone poles taking shots of the village against the sea and against the mountains.

There were men clamouring outside the gate of Granny O'Flaherty's house, but the door was closed and Paddy and Joe were standing in front of the gate; big stolid men, unsmiling, and you would think they had been dumb from birth because there wasn't a word out of them.

'Let us see the children,' and 'Where's Granny O'Flaherty?' 'Ah, come on have a heart, just one or two shots.'

To it all, Paddy and Joe just shook their heads, and they were so big and formidable-looking that none of the reporters even tried to go over the wall and get close to the house.

Then over the mountain road somebody shouted down to Paddy and Joe, 'Here they are now, Paddy.' Paddy looked up and they saw the two police cars coming down towards the village.

This set the reporters and the picture-taking men into a frenzy. They ran up towards the approaching cars, snapping from their knees and lying on their stomachs.

The police cars stopped a few hundred yards off, and about eight big policemen got out of them, with the Sergeant holding a paper and they started to walk down to the house, surrounded by the clamouring newspaper men and cameras. And now a very strange thing happened, because as the policemen came down the road, from all directions the men of the village started to come also, to the front of Granny O'Flaherty's house. They were big men and small men and old men, men with whiskers, and young clean-shaven ones, men with hats and men with caps, and men with no headgear at all, but they all had one thing in common; they were carrying sickles or scythes, or spades or sleans. Now, maybe it was time for them to go working with these things in the fields, but they would also be formidable weapons if anyone wanted to fight, and they also came and lined up on each side of Paddy and Joe, so that the whole wall was hidden by the bodies of at least thirty men, all of them armed, if that was the way you wanted to look at it.

Of course all this nearly drove the reporters into a

frenzy of delight. They couldn't have arranged this even if they had paid for it.

The Sergeant was taken aback at the sight. He lined his men up on the other side of the road opposite the village men. The policemen were wearing batons in black leather cases.

The Sergeant crossed over and spoke to Paddy.

'This is the warrant your mother was looking for,' he said, waving it in Paddy's face.

'Oh, I know nothing about that at all,' said Paddy.

'What are all these men doing here?' the Sergeant asked.

'They are just resting themselves,' said Paddy, 'before they go to work.'

The Sergeant looked along the line of men. Some of them were smoking pipes, some of them cigarettes. They all looked at him innocently.

'They don't look like that to me,' he said. 'Call out your mother.'

'Hey, Mother!' Paddy called. 'The Sergeant wants you.'

There was great fluttering and moving again amongst the reporters.

Inside, Granny said to Finn, 'You know what to do. They won't get into the house, but if there's a chance of it, out the back way and go into the house across the way. If he gets a warrant for that house we'll shift ye to another house. There's enough houses to keep changing into for a hundred years.'

She cackled again and opened the door, and Finn locked it after her and they went to the window and looked out.

On the appearance of Granny there was great activity among the reporters.

157

'What's this? What's this, Mrs O'Flaherty?' the Sergeant asked. 'Have you set up an armed conspiracy here, or what?'

'What do you mean?' she asked.

'All these men,' he said, 'with arms.'

'Is there a law against going to work and resting your back against a wall?' she asked.

'You know better than that,' he said. 'It's intimidation. You know I'm only carrying out the law. Here's the warrant. I'm serving it on you, and you are now in contempt of court.'

'You say these children are in the house. All right,' she said, 'why don't you go and look for yourself?'

The Sergeant got red in the face. He turned back towards his men. All the villagers shifted their positions. They came away from the wall and spread their legs and brought up their farm implements. The sun glittered on the steel of them.

The Sergeant stopped halfway and came back again.

'Look,' he said, 'think of my position. I wouldn't do anything about it at all, if I had my own way. You know that. Who wants to be unpopular? But there is the law and I must enforce it.'

'Who's stopping you?' she asked.

'Who's stopping me? Who's stopping me?' he asked the sky. He got control of himself. 'Won't you listen to the man who is really suffering over all this? Hey, Mister Morgan! Mister Morgan!' he called, waving his arm at the parked cars above. Everyone watched. There was great activity again as Uncle Toby came out of the car and walked down towards them.

Inside the house Finn and Derval saw his head as

158

he approached. Derval put her arm tightly around Finn's neck, and Finn's grip tightened on her waist.

Uncle Toby came through a battery of cameras. He had a handkerchief in his hand. He was wiping his eyes. He was really weeping. The reporters were delighted.

He stood in front of the gate and looked into Granny O'Flaherty's eyes. His hand was shaking. He looked pitiful. All were agreed on that.

'Mrs O'Flaherty,' he said, 'please give me back my children.'

'You never had any children,' said Granny. 'There isn't a single drop of your blood flowing in the veins of those children. You have no more claim on them than a man that would teach them in a school.'

'Mrs O'Flaherty,' he said. 'I was devoted to those children. Ask anyone and they will tell you. I was the husband of your daughter. I cherished her and I cherished them. Believe me.'

'If you weren't a tourist,' she said, 'and if there was nobody else here, I'd give you a piece of my mind. Man, I'd really tell you what I think of you.'

'That's enough now! That's enough,' said the Sergeant, 'and I've had enough. Get ready now men,' he called back to the police. 'If we are not allowed to do it the peaceful way, then we'll do it the hard way. Stand back, Mister Morgan.'

The police came forward taking their batons from their cases, and tightening the leather thongs about their wrists, pulling the straps of their caps under their chins and tightening those too. All the village men stiffened themselves and gripped their implements. The reporters and cameramen were going frantic.

159

The police moved forward.

The men moved forward.

It looked as if nothing on the face of the earth could stop it.

And then this car came up the road, very fast, and stopped between the police and the men, and Michael got out of it.

'Hello, Sergeant,' he said. 'Are you having trouble?'

'If we get trouble, we can take it,' said the Sergeant.

'You know the Judge,' said Michael, indicating the man getting out of the car. He was a thin man with a pleasant thin face and a balding head, but he didn't look like a judge. He was dressed as if he was going fishing on a lake, with big rubber boots of a green colour and a fishing jacket and a heavy hand-knitted sweater.

The Sergeant recognized him and came stiffly to attention. All the policemen did the same thing.

'Hello, Sergeant,' the Judge said. 'I want to lodge a complaint against this man. I was fishing peacefully on the loch, when he practically kidnapped me.'

'I'll charge him later, sir,' the Sergeant said, grinning, and then burst out, 'My God, we're glad to see you.'

The Judge looked around him.

'Hmm,' he said. 'I see that a situation has arisen.'

Michael said to Granny. 'I am Michael, Mrs O'Flaherty. Maybe the children spoke of me.'

The hard-looking face suddenly broke into a smile. She held out her hand. 'They did, indeed,' she said, 'and nothing but good.' She nearly broke his fingers with the handshake.

'Look,' he said. 'We can do something about this

160

peacefully. This is the Judge. I persuaded him to come along and talk. Will you let us in and we can discuss the whole thing? I can promise you that nobody will grab the children away from you. Judge, this is Mrs O'Flaherty.'

'I'm pleased to meet you, ma'am,' the Judge said. 'I'm only here in a private capacity, you understand, sort of *in loco parentis,* since, in a way, I am the legal father of the children.'

'You're as welcome as green grass,' she said. 'Paddy, go in and ready the priest's parlour. Come in! Come in! You'll have to excuse the way the house is.' She moved off with the Judge, holding his arm as if he was feeble.

'Bring the men back up the road, Sergeant,' Michael said. 'Do you think your side could go about their business now?' he asked Joe.

'Might we be needing them again?' Joe asked.

Michael grinned.

'I don't think so,' he said, 'but if you are, I personally will give you the beck.'

'Fine,' said Joe.

'Mister Morgan,' said Michael, 'if you wouldn't mind waiting at the car, I'll send for you. I promise that you will see the children.'

'I'd better,' said Uncle Toby. 'They are mine by law.'

'The law will look after them,' said Michael, and then turned and went towards the house, and was not surprised when he reached the kitchen that Derval ran towards him and he had to bend down and take her in his arms.

Chapter Twenty-one

'All right,' the Judge said. 'Bring them in.'

Michael went into the kitchen. The Judge looked around at the room. There was a small brown table at which he was sitting and soft-bottom chairs, ornaments on the mantelpiece and many pictures of the O'Flahertys from various lands, when they were married, when they were being baptized.

Michael said to the children, 'Don't be afraid. He is a good man. Answer any questions he asks you.'

'He better be nice to them,' said Granny.

'He will,' said Michael.

'Will you be there?' Finn asked.

'I will,' said Michael.

'We will go in, so,' said Finn, catching Derval's hand.

Derval looked at Granny O'Flaherty.

'It will be all right,' Granny said grimly. 'We are here behind you, aren't we?'

Derval nodded.

The Judge watched them as they came in. He was interested in the boy. He was thin, he saw. His face was closed. Freckles and red hair and a determined chin. He didn't look like a troublemaker. They stood in front of him. The girl had her finger in her mouth. She would be most endearing, the Judge thought, but I mustn't let her charm me.

'Finn,' he said. 'This is all most unofficial. Strictly

speaking I shouldn't be here at all. I should be fishing. Things like this should take place in Judge's Chambers. Legally I'm a sort of father to you. If you would think of me that way. Don't feel that I am your enemy. I'm not. Do you understand this?'

'I think I do,' said Finn.

'Do you feel that you have done a great deed, running away from home, crossing the sea, making hares out of the police, and triumphantly arriving at your destination?'

'Oh, no,' said Finn.

'But you should,' said the Judge. 'It was a remarkable thing to do.'

'But I didn't do it,' said Finn.

'What do you mean?' the Judge asked.

'Well, it was all the other people,' said Finn. 'All the people who helped us; Poll, and Tom and Mickser, and Moses, and Michael here. If it wasn't for them we would have been caught long ago.'

'I see,' said the Judge. 'So you hadn't much to do with it, really.'

'Oh, no,' said Finn sincerely. 'How could I do it if we hadn't been helped? Look at Derval. She is very young and she is a girl and look at the way she kept going. If she didn't keep going like that we could never have travelled. You see. It wasn't that much to do with me.'

'I see,' said the Judge. 'If you are returned to your Uncle Toby, what would you do, Finn?'

Finn thought of this.

'I would run away again the first chance I got,' he said.

'And you would bring Derval with you?' the Judge asked.

'Yes,' said Finn, his jaw tight.

'Why?' the Judge asked.

Finn thought over this.

'Well,' he said, 'just because.'

'Uncle Toby beat Finn,' said Derval suddenly.

'Derval,' said Finn shaking her by the shoulder.

'Yes, he did,' she said. 'I don't care. He beat him and beat him and beat him, and Finn didn't cry, but I did.'

'Your uncle Toby was cruel to you?' the Judge asked.

'It's not that,' said Finn, shifting uncomfortably.

'Yes, he did,' said Derval. 'All the time. He never let him alone. I hate Uncle Toby. He was nasty to Finn.'

'Will you shut up, Derval,' said Finn.

'If you don't talk, she certainly will,' said the Judge.

'It's love,' said Finn, in a burst. 'Children should have someone to love them. Not me, but girls like Derval. You see? And I knew that Granny would be cracked about her if I could get to her. Just like Mother and Father were. You see? Not me, because I'm big and I can take care of myself. But it's Derval. She has to have somebody. And there was nobody. Uncle Toby didn't care for her. Do you understand?'

The Judge was looking at him. His face wasn't closed now. It was very open and appealing. He began to understand the attraction he had for Michael, who had gone on his holidays and at his own expense had found out many pertinent things, just because he had liked Finn.

'In my job, Finn,' he said, 'we come up against a lot of sadness and injustice. That's what we are for, to try and unravel such things. We will endeavour to unravel this one. You may take it that I understand. We are

164

going to talk to Uncle Toby now. You don't have to be present unless you want to.'

'I don't want to,' said Finn. 'If you don't mind.'

'All right,' he said. 'Michael, see them down and then bring me Uncle Toby.'

'You're nice,' said Derval to the Judge.

'Thank you, Derval,' he said, laughing, 'but it isn't everybody would agree with you.'

He watched them out.

Michael said to Granny, 'I'm going to bring in Uncle Toby now.'

'In my house? Never,' said Granny.

'Look,' said Michael, 'There is law. People can't keep fighting the law for ever. Just this once go along with the law. Have a look at it, and if you don't like the results, sure you can start the war again.'

'You're a policeman,' she said. 'How can you be a policeman and be helping the children like you did?'

Michael saw Finn looking at him with the question in his eyes too. Michael winked at him.

'Ah, but,' he said, 'I was a policeman on holiday.'

He saw Finn take this in.

'Can I bring him in?' he asked.

'All right,' said Granny. 'We can disinfect the house afterwards.'

Michael laughed and went out. Granny ushered Finn and Derval out the back door.

The Judge looked at Uncle Toby. He was a respectable-looking man with a worried forehead. He still had a handkerchief in his hand to dab at his eyes.

'Please sit down,' said the Judge. Toby sat.

'Mister Morgan,' he said. 'You made the children Wards of Court. Why?'

'To get them back, of course,' said Uncle Toby.

165

'You see what has happened now. This old lady holding off a police force with armed men. Wasn't I right to do it? I had to have the law.'

'Why?' the Judge asked.

'What else could I do?' Toby asked.

'Why did they run away?' the Judge asked.

'You've seen that boy Finn,' said Toby, suddenly getting angry. 'A headstrong, wayward boy, ready for any mischief.'

'He didn't appear that way to me,' said the Judge.

'Ah, but you don't know him,' said Toby. 'He is deceitful and dishonest, a delinquent in sheep's clothing, that's what that boy is. The mental agony and torture that he has imposed on me and on that little girl!'

'This was your only reason?' the Judge asked.

'What other reason is there?' Toby asked.

'It could have been because you loved them so much that you wanted them back,' the Judge said.

'There are limits to love,' said Toby. 'You saw the boy. How could anybody but his own mother love him?'

'So why didn't you let him go?' the Judge asked.

'I have a duty to their dead mother,' said Toby.

'And what about the legacy?' the Judge asked.

'What legacy?' Toby said, after a pause.

'Come, come, Mister Morgan. There is a large legacy left in trust for the children, by a deceased grand-uncle. Why didn't you say anything about this when you made them Wards of Court?'

'But this comes as a great surprise to me,' said Uncle Toby.

'Come, come, Mister Morgan,' said the Judge. 'The information came from America, and only then your

166

employer, Mister Purdon, admitted that he was the solicitor contacted, and that he had informed you.'

Uncle Toby was left without words.

'Also,' said the Judge, 'when this issue comes to court, as it must, there will be some witnesses called who will give a rather bad impression of the way you dealt with these children.'

'That's not true,' said Toby in anguish.

'I'm afraid it is true, sir,' said Michael. 'I spoke to some of them. Three are willing to testify that they were shocked at the way you treated the children and particularly the boy Finn. They are most indignant. They said that they would be willing to come to court and testify.'

'There are Judases in every society,' said Uncle Toby, pounding the table with his fist.

'Mister Morgan,' said the Judge. 'I have some knowledge of the law and of justice. I will give you advice, completely unofficial. If I were you, and to save a lot of things coming out in the court that might distress you, I would apply to have the children discharged as Wards of Court.'

Uncle Toby thought over this.

'But it's not fair!' he wailed. 'Where is the justice of it all?'

'Justice always seems to have two sides,' said the Judge.

They watched the struggle going on in Uncle Toby's face.

'All this has cost me a lot,' he said. 'Most of my savings!'

If this was an appeal, it met two blank faces.

'One hears about these things,' Uncle Toby said.

'Justice is blind they said, and I didn't believe it, but now I know.'

'May I suggest,' said the Judge, 'that out there you have representatives of the Press of many countries who have become caught up in this story. It would be a fitting climax, if you were to go out to them, and make a statement in your own words, that you are willing to sacrifice your own feelings for the welfare of the children, and that you are permitting them to stay with their grandmother and withdraw the declaration making them Wards of Court. Think of this. It will be such a noble gesture. I imagine it will be appreciated by millions of readers, and you could emerge as – eh – somewhat of a hero.'

They watched his face. They saw many emotions sweeping across it, anger, frustration, greed, hatred of them. For a few moments his face was naked, and then he decided to shed a few more tears, and Michael relaxed the muscles of his stomach.

'You have left me no alternative,' said Uncle Toby. 'I will adopt your suggestion.'

If only I could cheer, Michael thought.

Toby rose to his feet.

'I will for ever hold in doubt the laws of this country,' he said with dignity. 'I would never believe that a distinguished member of the judiciary could dispense cruel laws in the parlour of an obscure peasant. Good day, gentlemen.'

They looked at one another as he went out the door. Then the Judge moved quickly to the window and pulled back the lace curtain discreetly, and Michael ran down to the kitchen.

Toby was just going out the door.

Granny was peeping in the back door.

Michael pulled it open.

He caught Derval up in his arms.

'It's over!' he shouted. 'It's over. You belong to Granny. Here, take her!' putting her into Granny's arms. 'Come on over and listen, Finn.' He pushed Finn over to the other window. He had a hand on his shoulder.

Toby had gathered his audience. They loved him.

'Moved by feelings of love,' Toby was sounding off, 'and at the expense of much wrenching to my own heart, I have decided to withdraw the children from being Wards of Court and permit them to remain with their blood-relations.'

They didn't listen any more. Finn's eyes were glistening.

'You did it, Finn!' said Michael. 'You did it!'

'Yah-hah-hoo,' shouted Uncle Paddy.

'Yah-hah-hoo,' shouted Uncle Joe.

And for the very first time Michael saw Finn really smiling.

Chapter Twenty-two

Finn was with Uncle Paddy and Uncle Joe. They were getting the ponies ready and he had the donkey. There were panniers on the back of the donkey and they were preparing to go up the mountain to the bog.

They were attracted by the sight of Derval coming out of the house hauling Granny O'Flaherty by the hand.

'I want to go to the strand,' Derval was saying. 'Just to see. You must come, Granny.'

'But how can I?' she was asking. 'I have to get the dinner, feed the pigs.'

'Just once,' Derval was saying, pulling away at her.

'Wouldn't the people say I am mad?' said Granny. 'Going to the strand in the morning! Be off with you.'

'Ah, please, Granny; please, Granny,' Derval said.

'No,' said Granny. 'No, I tell you.'

But all the same, she was being pulled forward.

'I'll help you to get the dinner, afterwards, but now we go to the strand,' said Derval.

'Only for five minutes, so, you hear?' Granny shouted. 'Just for five minutes, you hear?'

'Just for a little while,' said Derval. 'We can pick shells and we can paddle and look at the little crabs.'

'Oh, my God,' groaned Granny.

'Granny O'Flaherty has met her match,' said Paddy.

'And she loves it,' said Joe.

The three of them looked at one another and laughed, and started to mount the animals.

A selected list of titles available from Macmillan Children's Books

The prices shown below are correct at the time of going to press.
However, Macmillan Publishers reserves the right to show new retail prices
on covers, which may differ from those previously advertised.

Elizabeth Laird

A Little Piece of Ground	978-0-330-43743-1	£5.99
Crusade	978-0-330-45699-9	£6.99
Jake's Tower	978-0-330-39803-9	£5.99
Kiss the Dust	978-0-230-01431-2	£5.99
Oranges in No Man's Land	978-0-330-44558-0	£4.99
Paradise End	978-0-330-39999-9	£4.99
Red Sky in the Morning	978-0-330-44290-9	£5.99
Secrets of the Fearless	978-0-330-43466-9	£5.99
The Garbage King	978-0-330-41502-6	£5.99
Lost Riders	978-0-330-45209-0	£5.99
The Witching Hour	978-0-230-73679-5	£12.99

All Pan Macmillan titles can be ordered from our website,
www.panmacmillan.com, or from your local bookshop
and are also available by post from:

Bookpost, PO Box 29, Douglas, Isle of Man IM99 1BQ
Credit cards accepted. For details:
Telephone: 01624 677237
Fax: 01624 670923
Email: bookshop@enterprise.net
www.bookpost.co.uk

Free postage and packing in the United Kingdom